COMBUST

A Devil Chasers' MC Romance

L Wilder

This book is a work of fiction. Some of the places named in the book are actual places found in Paris, TN. The names, characters, brands, and incidents are either the product of the author's imagination or are used fictitiously. The author acknowledges the trademarked status and owners of various products and locations referenced in this work of fiction, which have been used without permission. The publication or use of these trademarks is not authorized, associated with, or sponsored by the trademark owners.

 Warning: This book is intended for readers 18 years or older due to bad language, violence and explicit sex scenes.

Editor: Brooke Asher
www.facebook.com/pages/Brooke-Asher-Editing/517436751724676

Cover by: Carrie at
http://cheekycovers.com/

Cover Photographer: Randy Sewell
www.facebook.com/rlsmodels?fref=ts

DEDICATION

To My Readers

Your support through messages and posts has touched me more than you will ever know. Thank you all for making the Devil Chasers' series such a great success.

PROLOGUE

ONE MONTH EARLIER

"AFTER REVIEWING THE accusations against you, Ms. Sanders, I have decided to suspend you from the residency until further notice," Mr. Edwards said coldly. He glared at me through his reading glasses, disgust apparent in his eyes. His hands were hidden in the pockets of his freshly ironed lab coat. He towered over me with his broad shoulders, intimidating me for the first time since I'd met him. He'd always been so nice to me, encouraging me to push myself harder. Seeing him look at me with such disapproval hurt more than I'd expected.

"I don't understand," I told him. "What accusations? I honestly don't know what you're talking about."

"There are several things actually. The allegations against you just keep growing, Ms. Sanders. It looks like you have been a very busy young lady." He crossed his arms, and I felt myself cower under his daunting glare.

"What things?" I asked.

"There is evidence that you have cheated on multiple exams. A disturbing report that you mishandled distribution of medication which caused one of our patients to have multiple seizures, almost killing her. If that isn't enough, it seems that you're having relations with one of our married surgeons. I am extremely disappointed in you. You've made some very poor decisions, Ms. Sanders." He said my name with such anger, such repulsion. None of what he said was true, but I knew he wasn't going to listen to my defense. Everything I'd worked for was slipping right through my fingertips over a bunch of lies. My mind was racing, and a tightness was building in my chest. I couldn't look at him, so I glanced around his office, trying to ground myself. I needed to say something, to try to fix things, but I didn't know where to start. I couldn't understand how it'd all happened. I'd always tried to do the right thing. I'd been totally dedicated to becoming a doctor, letting everything else in my life fall second.

I'd given everything I had to succeeding, and I would've never done anything to jeopardize my career. Something just wasn't right. I knew deep down in my gut that Jason Thomas was behind it, but I had no way to prove it. I didn't know how he'd done it, but I had to find a way to clear my name. I just had to. Being a doctor had been my dream for as long as I could remember, and I wasn't going to let some rich prick take it away from me.

I turned my head back to Mr. Edwards, looking him straight in the eye, and said, "Sir, none of this is true. Not one word. I know you don't believe me, but I will find a way to prove it to you." I grabbed my bag and pulled the strap over my shoulder, preparing to leave the room. Before I left, I looked back to him and said, "I am the strongest student in this residency, and we both know it. I will find out who is behind all of this, and I will make it right."

Without waiting for his response, I walked out of his office. The hallway was just a blur as the tears filled my eyes. I kept my eyes locked on the floor as I made my way into the restroom. After locking the door, I rested my back against the wall and slid down to the cool marble tiles. The tears were flowing freely, and there wasn't a damn thing I could do to stop them. I felt so lost. My life was spinning out of control, and I didn't know what to do to stop it.

I sat there feeling sorry for myself for several minutes before the anger began to rise in the pit of my stomach. I wiped the tears from my eyes and lifted myself off of the floor. I brushed off my pants and walked over to the sink. I splashed cold water on my face, trying to erase the trail of tears that crossed my cheeks. I looked at myself in the mirror, and I couldn't believe what I saw. I was stronger than the person staring back at me. I wasn't the kind of person that let something like that tear me apart. I needed to get home and get my shit together. No one stopped me as I rushed out of the hospital.

I called Steven as soon as I got into my car, and thankfully, he was sitting on my front step waiting for me when I pulled into my driveway. Just knowing he was there gave me a sense of relief. He'd been my best friend for almost six years. He'd moved into the house next door to me when I was seventeen. He was an English author who moved to here to focus on his next book. We really were an odd pair. I was always so reserved, watching every word that came out of my mouth, while he was the smartass, always giving everybody hell. I honestly didn't know how we got along so well, but we worked. I felt lucky to have him. I'd never have been able to survive my mother's death if he hadn't been there for me. I'd spent two years watching her fight a losing battle against ovarian cancer, and it was heartbreaking. It was painful to watch her try to hide her suffering, but I refused to leave her side. When she finally passed away, I was devastated. Steven was my rock. He was always there for me, pulling me out of my deep depression.

I grabbed my stuff and got out of the car, heading towards him while I tried to put on a brave face. I didn't know why I even bothered. He knew me better than anyone. I glanced over to him and tried to smile.

"Bloody hell, woman! You look awful," he told me as he grimaced. "What's going on with you?"

I let out a deep sigh and walked past him, unlocking my front door. "My life just went to shit. That's what's going on," I told him as I dropped my things on the floor and headed into the kitchen.

"How's that?" he asked with concern, as he sat down on one of the stools by my kitchen counter.

"Mr. Edwards called me into his office before rounds. He told me that he was suspending me from the residency program because apparently I cheated on my finals, almost killed a patient, and I am screwing one of the surgeons."

"That's bullshit!" he snapped. "Didn't you tell him it wasn't true?"

"I told him, but I could tell he wasn't listening. He'd already completely made up his mind about me. Until I can prove it, he's going to keep thinking I'm lying."

"Somebody is doing their best to make sure you don't complete the residency program," he said flatly.

"Tell me about it."

"You think Jason has something to do with this?" Steven asked.

"I have no doubt in my mind that he's behind all of it. He's gone to a lot of trouble. I just can't figure out why he's so determined to ruin me like this."

"He doesn't like the fact that you're a better doctor than him, Ana. He'd always been on top until you came around, and he doesn't like to be second. I'm sure that he isn't very fond of you right now."

"None of this makes any sense. I don't even know why he bothered to ask me out. I thought he genuinely liked me," I told him.

I'd been surprised the day he approached me in the lunchroom. He was so sweet, almost bashful, as he'd asked me to dinner, but I'd quickly turned him down. It wasn't that I didn't find him attractive; he was handsome in his own way. At that time, I'd had no interest in starting anything up with any man. I hadn't been on a real date since my mother had died, and I didn't see that changing anytime soon. I was completely focused on becoming a doctor, and I didn't want or need any distractions. I was determined, and I wasn't going to let anyone or anything stand in my way. Regardless, he wasn't happy about me turning him down. After that, things shifted between us.

At first, I didn't even recognize the difference in him. But shortly after our quarterly exams, everything changed. Jason began glaring at me during class, making me feel on edge. Then, he started interrupting me whenever I tried to make my diagnosis during rounds. He would look over to me and smirk whenever he was given credit for acknowledging a medical problem first. It had all really begun to irritate me, but I didn't know how to stop him. I'd noticed a few mistakes he'd made with his patient's medication, but no one listened when I'd tried to point out the errors. They'd always seemed to take his side whenever I'd brought it up. I'd even tried talking to him about everything, but that had just seemed to make things worse.

Strange phone calls from the hospital had started coming at random times throughout the night. Each time I'd seen the number on my phone, I'd assumed it was someone calling me into work, or that there was an issue with a patient. Occasionally, it was one of the other residents calling to check in, but those calls were few and far between. Usually when I answered, no one even spoke. Whoever was calling would sit there without saying a word and just breathe into the phone.

The phone calls had just been the beginning, though. Threatening letters were randomly put in my mailbox or my car. Then, someone hacked into all of my email accounts, sending awful emails to everyone I knew. Yes, the problem had been escalating, but I'd never expected to lose my job. It had been a bombshell, and I had no doubt that it was all related.

"I don't know what his true intentions were, but now we know it couldn't have been good," Steven told me as he walked over to me. "Do you think this has anything to do with Jason's patients you were asking around about?"

"I have no idea, but I don't think there's any way I can find out now."

He wrapped his arms around me and said, "I'm sorry, doll. I wish I could make this all go away."

"What am I going to do? I've worked so hard for this, and now…." I couldn't continue. I rested my head on his shoulder and cried for the second time. I really hated crying. It made me feel weak and needy, but I couldn't stop myself. Steven held me until I was able to get myself together. I pulled myself away from his embrace and said, "I'm sorry about that. I'm okay. I'll figure something out."

"Stop it, Ana. You're not alone in this. *We* will figure this out, and you know your dad will do anything he can to help," he told me.

"I'm not going to say anything to him… yet. I need a few days to try to figure all this out, and I don't want him to worry," I replied.

"We will find a way to fix this, Ana. You've worked too hard. I won't let them take your dream away," he assured me.

"Thank you, Steven," I said as I wiped the tears from my face.

"Why don't we go have a few drinks? Take your mind off of things for a bit."

"Not tonight. I just want to take a hot bath and go to bed," I told him.

"Do you want me to stay here with you? Maybe watch a movie or something?" he asked.

"No, thanks, but I think I'd rather just be alone," I said with a heavy sigh.

"Alright, but I'll be down at the pub if you need me," he said as he leaned over and gave me a kiss on the cheek.

"It's called a *bar*, Steven. We're in Kentucky. There are no pubs in Kentucky," I told him with a smile.

"It's all in one's perspective, my dear," he said, giving me a wink.

I shook my head as I watched him walk out the front door. It'd only be a matter of time before he had some poor woman swooning over him. It cracked me up how they all fell for him. He didn't even have to work for it. As soon as they heard his English accent, he had them eating out of the palm of his hand. They always found him so charming, with his wavy, dark brown hair and hazel eyes. Those beautiful eyes got them every time. They drew the ladies in like bees to honey. The women just couldn't help themselves. The minute he mentioned that he was an author, they were completely hooked… and it didn't help matters that he was devastatingly handsome. Those poor women didn't stand a chance.

There was a time that I'd actually wondered what it would've been like if we ever tried to be more than just friends. The truth was… he was more like a brother to me. I knew that sounded cliché, but it was true. I didn't think I could ever see him as anything more. We kept each other going whenever the world around us got all screwed up. As always, he had been there for me again when I'd needed him. I had no idea what was going to happen with my residency, but I knew at least I wouldn't have to go through it alone.

CHAPTER 1
SHEPPARD

THE BLACK DIAMONDS are closing in. We've been doing a pretty good job of holding them off, but they are determined to take us down and have more men than us. When I notice that my president, Bishop, is under attack, I don't take the time to think. I quickly step out from the protective barrier of the barge's steel side rail. The smell of gun smoke fills the air as bullets fly past me. I begin to advance towards my target, oblivious of the danger that surrounds me. I only have one thing on my mind… removing my target. The two men continue to fire in Bishop's direction, and I know I have to do something before it's too late.

There is no way I would let anything happen to him. He'd been the one person that was able to pull me free from the darkness and make me feel human again. I had been a changed man when I'd returned from Afghanistan. Not only did I have shrapnel embedded into three-fourths of my body, I'd had a severe case of post-traumatic stress disorder. I was a man haunted by the demons of war, unable to escape the dreadful thoughts inside my head. Without Bishop's help, I'm not sure what would have happened to me. He'd encouraged me to join the Devil Chasers, become part of their family... their brotherhood. They'd helped me fight back the nightmares and find my way back to reality. I owed them my life, and I would do anything I could to protect them.

I take my shot and smile with satisfaction as the first man drops to the ground. The man standing beside him watches his partner fall and quickly turns, pointing his gun in my direction. Surprise crosses his face as he sees me standing there in the open. Before he has a chance to react, I fire my weapon, killing him instantly. Relief washes over me as I watch his limp body crash to the ground.

I should have moved... taken cover... something, but I hesitate. It costs me. Searing pain explodes through my chest as the first bullet forces its way through my flesh. The impact of the second bullet is so strong that I lose my balance, falling over the side of the barge and colliding into the water below. I'd always heard about the water being rough by the dam, but I never dreamed that it could be this strong. When the raging current pulls me under, I can hear the roar of the water as it rushes through turbines at the spillway.

My body rips through the water, forcing water into my nose and mouth. I feel myself being pulled deeper into the water, and my mind races with panic. I am trained for situations like this, but the two bullet wounds make it difficult to pull myself together. I begin kicking my legs, trying my best to make it to the surface. Each time I reach the top of the rapid water, the current catches my legs and pulls me back under. The sporadic gasps of air are making me desperate, but I refuse to die gracefully.

My adrenaline finally kicks in, and I no longer feel any pain. I manage to free myself of my heavy leather jacket, knowing it is only dragging me down. This is no time for sentiment. I am on the verge of losing consciousness and fighting against the current is draining all of my strength. I am getting close to my breaking point. I reach the surface again and take a frantic, deep breath. Thankfully, my military training takes over. I know I need to stop and let the current do all of the work. It may carry me down a few miles, but it will eventually get me to shore.

I struggle to keep my head above the water as the current continues to pull me under. The icy water is starting to make my limbs numb, and I'm finding it hard to stay awake. My heart races in desperation as I try to keep myself from passing out. I can see a small group of houses along the shore, and I pray that I have enough strength to make it to land. My body is just about to give as my feet begin to drag along the bottom of the lake. I try to stand, but my legs are too weak. After several attempts, I am finally able to get my footing and begin the long trek to the shoreline. My clothes and my body feel like lead as I trudge through the riverbed. As I finally reach the edge of the sand, my body drops to the ground in exhaustion, and everything goes black.

CHAPTER 2

ANA

I CRINGE WHEN the telephone rings, waking me from my nap. I almost don't even answer, but I decide to take the risk. I look down at the screen, and I'm relieved when I see that it's my father. He wants to take me into town later today for some shopping, so he can get a few things for the farm. He says he's running low on feed for the horses, but I know it is just an excuse to get me out of the house. It's been over a week since I've been anywhere, and I do need to get a few groceries, so I agree to go. It's a "two birds with one stone" sort of thing.

After a quick cup of coffee, I decide to take one of my walks down by the lake. It is the only place I still feel a level of freedom. It is my one true escape from the hell I've been going through over the past month. I keep praying that things will get better, but they never do.

I grab my hoodie and scarf and head out my back door. The cool air nips at my nose, but fortunately it isn't as cold as it usually is in February. As I step outside, the light from the sun makes its way through the trees, warming my face. I love days like this. This time of year, the weather changes at the drop of a hat. I know I need to take advantage of these beautiful days while I can.

I follow the gravel trail that leads down to the water and then begin my hike along the rocky edge. I love listening to the birds chirping as I walk along the trail. Taking a deep breath of fresh air, I can't hold back my smile. I know spring is just around the corner. Soon, the leaves will start to change, bringing the lake back to life.

I've barely reached the water when I notice something lying along the rocks down by the dock. There is something familiar about its shape, leading me to step closer. I quickly realize that it is a person… a man lying face down in the water. I rush over to him, immediately filled with a sense of foreboding.

When I reach his limp body, I see that his head is barely out of the water. I quickly drop down to my knees, lifting his head, and place two fingers against the side of his neck, searching for a pulse. I don't feel anything, but something inside me urges me on, telling me this man isn't dead. Everything that had happened to me over the past month seemed to vanish at that moment. With newfound confidence, I feel like I'm a doctor again. I press my fingers firmly into his neck, determined to find his pulse. I breathe deep and try to concentrate on feeling something… anything. Relief washes over me when I finally find it. I kneel down in the icy water and the cold wind sends chills through my body. I plunge my hands and arms into the murky, dark water and reach under his shoulders. Bending and locking my hands under his arms, I wedge my feet in the mud and with all my strength, pull. We both fly backwards, his body landing hard on top of me, stunning me with its weight. I roll him off of me and quickly examine the body. Two bullet wounds catch my attention first, but they have to wait.

He shows no signs of breathing, so I tilt his head back and pull open his mouth by his chin. I stare down at his rugged, masculine face covered in cuts and wonder what had happened to him. I kneel by his side and lean over, covering his mouth with mine. I exhale, filling his lungs with my breath. I repeat this ten times and then recheck for any signs of breathing. There's nothing, but I'm not giving up. I continue to give him CPR until he coughs and jerks to life. I roll him over onto his side to help get the water out.

A sense of pride fills my soul as I watch him take another breath. Seeing the rise and fall of his chest makes me feel more alive than I have in my entire life. At that moment, I wonder who had really saved whom. I grab my cell phone and call my dad. Luckily, he lives just down the road. It will still take him a few minutes to get here, so I remove my hoodie and press it to the gunshot wounds. I have to try to slow the bleeding while I wait for my father.

A look of utter shock crosses my father's face as he approaches us. He isn't the kind of man to turn his back on someone in need, so I have no doubt that he will do all he can to help. I watch as he tries to make sense of what is happening. He kneels down and lifts my hoodie.

He lets out a deep breath as he glances over the wounds on the man's chest. He shakes his head from side to side and then looks over to me.

"You have to help me," I plead.

"What exactly do you want me to do here, Ana?" my father asks.

"He's going to die if we don't do something," I tell him.

"I don't know, Ana. Someone wanted this guy dead bad enough to shoot him twice and toss him into the lake. He had to be in some kind of serious trouble, and the last thing we need around here is more trouble. If this goes bad, you'll never get back your residency at the hospital. You can't be linked to a dead body, Ana."

I know he's right, but I have to try to help. I want to become a doctor so I can save lives, but there is more to this than that. This isn't just the urge to save someone's life. There is something about the look on this man's face that grabs me. I can't explain it. I just have to help him. I have to.

"Please, Daddy. Just help me get him inside. I'll take care of the rest," I beg.

He walks over to the shed and grabs the old wheelbarrow. He runs his hands through his silver hair as he walks back over to me and says, "It'll be hard to get him up the hill; he's heavy."

"Thanks, Daddy," I reply, bending down to grab the stranger's feet. My dad reaches under his shoulders, and together we carefully lift him up into the wheelbarrow. His head tosses from side to side as we push him up the path that leads to the house.

"Where do you want me to put him?" he asks.

"Let's try to get him to my room. I'll need your help getting these wet clothes off of him."

"I think you've got more to worry about than a few wet clothes. He really needs a hospital," he warns.

"You know we can't take him there. Besides, there's no time," I plead. "He's not going to make it much longer. Let me see what I can do to help him first. If there's nothing I can do, we'll think of something else." As much as I know he needs a hospital, I just can't risk it. I can't trust anyone there. The entire hospital has been corrupted by the Thomas family and their money. Jason's father is the chief surgeon on staff, and he's known for being tough. No one dares to ask questions. I know there is something going on… some kind of secret, but I can't put my finger on what it is. Over the past few months, strange things had happened in the hospital. When I'd started making inquiries, Jason and his father had done everything in their power to shut me out and make things difficult for me. They didn't want anyone meddling in their plans… especially me. With all of that going on, I just can't risk taking a stranger there. I only hope that I have what it takes to save him.

"I'll work on the clothes, and you make a list of things you might need from town, and I'll go get them," my father says determinedly.

"Thanks. I really appreciate this," I tell him.

"Just be careful, honey. We don't know anything about this guy," he warns, never letting me forget that

I'm still his little girl.

"I will. Just hurry. We don't have much time," I urge him as I head to my room, preparing myself for what lay ahead.

CHAPTER 3

SHEPPARD

SO THIS IS what dying is like.... I see the face of an angel as I'm lifted out of the water. I try to focus on her as I'm haphazardly tossed into some kind of metal wagon. My lifeless body sways from side to side as I'm carried up some kind of rocky hill. I can hear her beautiful voice calling out to me, urging me to stay. I want to answer, but no words come out. Her hand brushes across my face, calming me, but shadows are closing in. There isn't anything else I can do to stop it. It's getting more and more difficult to breathe, and I can feel the life slowly drifting out of my body. She whispers in my ear. Her words are so soft, so gentle. There's something about her voice.... She's like a light, beckoning me through the darkness. I want to go to her, but the pull is too strong. I can't get to her.

I feel myself being lifted again and placed on something soft, and my body sighs with relief. I try once again to open my eyes. I need to see my angel one last time before I go. Something in my gut tells me she's the only one that can release me from my nightmare. I fight with all my remaining strength, but I feel myself drifting away from consciousness. I panic. I have to see her… have to know that she is really here. I force my eyes open, and I can barely make out her face as she leans over me. Her piercing green eyes command me to stay with her, and for the first time since I landed in that water, I actually feel hope.

I try to take a deep breath, but the agony is just too much. The pain sears through my body, burning me to my soul. I can see her lips moving as she tries to talk to me, to reassure me, but it isn't enough. I can't fight the darkness any longer. As much as I want to stay here with her, there is nothing more I can do. I have no more fight left in me. I close my eyes, and the darkness devours me.

CHAPTER 4

ANA

MY HEART ACHES as I look at the stranger's motionless body lying in my bed. My room doesn't even look like the same place. I've done my best to prepare for the upcoming surgery, disinfecting everything he may come in contact with. Dad has already removed his clothes and laid a sheet over his lower body. He helped me clean and wash him up, removing all the muck from the lake. I wipe his chest down with betadine as I carefully examine his wounds. I am relieved to find that they aren't as bad as I'd thought. I'll be able to remove the bullets without being too invasive.

"He's lost a lot of blood, Ana. There's no way he's going to make it through this."

"I'm not giving up on him yet, Dad. I'm going to need some antibiotics," I tell him.

"I'll see if Sue can help us out. She'll ask questions, but we can trust her. I'll see if she has any painkillers, too. He's going to be in a world of hurt if he wakes up. Call me if you think of anything else."

I know that my dad has been dating Sue for several

months, but he hasn't actually told me about it. The silly man lights up like a Christmas tree every time he talks about her, though. She runs a small clinic in town, and she's a really great doctor. I know she'll have everything we would need. I only hope that she'll give it to us.

I grab the IV kit and one saline drip from my medical bag and walk over to him. I gently place the IV needle into his arm, so I can start a blood transfusion. He will need the extra blood before I can try to remove the bullets from his chest. My blood type is O negative, so I don't have to worry about him rejecting it. I give him just enough to stabilize him for the surgery, and then I remove the line from my arm. I replace the tubing so I can attach the saline drip. It will help increase his fluids and make it easier to give him his medications when they get here.

After scrubbing my hands with disinfectant, I reach for my scalpel and begin removing the first bullet from his chest. I'm immediately surprised at how shallow the bullet wound is. Luckily, something must have blocked it from going any deeper into his skin. A few more inches and it would have punctured his lung, leaving no chance that he would have survived.

The second bullet is much more difficult to remove. It is lodged in his lower abdomen, extremely close to his left kidney. After a great deal of work and two deep incisions, I'm finally able to extract it. He'll have a major scar, but it will heal with time. Thankfully, neither bullet struck any of his vital organs.

I'm still stitching him up when my dad walks back

into the room. "Got the antibiotics. Sue wasn't sure what you would need, so she sent everything she could. She also sent two extra saline drips and extra pain medication."

"Thanks, Daddy. I owe her one. Just put them on the dresser," I tell him as I tie off the last stitch. I don't have any time to waste. He needs to start the antibiotics before infection sets in. I inject the medication into his IV along with a dose of morphine that Sue sent. Dad is right. He's going to be in pain when he wakes up… if he wakes up. That thought scares me a little. I don't quite understand my overwhelming need to save this man, but I plan to do whatever it takes to keep him alive.

"How's he doing?" Dad asks.

"Better than I thought, actually. His blood pressure is low, but his heart rate is strong. He should improve quickly now that the bleeding has stopped. Hopefully the meds will help with the rest," I explain as I check the IV.

"So, what happens now?"

"We wait," I explain. "It's going to be awhile before we know anything. You can go home, Dad. There's no reason for you to stay. I doubt he'll even wake up for several days. I'll call you if something changes."

"I'm not leaving you alone, Ana. I wouldn't feel right leaving you alone with this guy," he huffs.

"Don't be silly. Go home and get some rest. Seriously, I'll be fine," I tell him. I motion my hand over to the lifeless man resting in my bed and say, "It's not like he's going to wake up any time soon. I'll keep an eye on things and let you know how it's going."

"What about Steven? You planning on telling him about your little project?" he asks, pointing over to the bed.

"Hmm… I'm not sure what I'm going to do. Let's just see how this all plays out."

"Ana…. Be careful," he warns.

"I will," I promise.

"I'll be back in the morning to see how things are going. Just so you know, I don't feel good about this," he says. "I'll call later to check on you."

I nod and watch as he turns to walk out of the room. I should be nervous about being left alone with a stranger like this, but I actually feel relief as my dad's truck pulls out of the driveway. Then again, it's not like he's going far. The farm is just a few miles down the road. Steven still lives next door, so I have plenty of help if I need it.

I sit on the edge of the bed and take a minute to look around the room. It's a complete disaster. There are bloodstains everywhere, and I know it will take me all night to clean up the mess. My attention is drawn away from the havoc in my room to the handsome man that lies in my bed, fighting for his life. I quietly watch as his chest rises and falls with each breath he takes. I lean over and run my fingers through his sandy brown hair. My eyes roam over the muscles of his chest and arms, while I try to make sense of all the tattoos scattered over his body. They're really quite beautiful and filled with intricate detail. It's like they're telling me a story… his story. I wonder if he might explain them all to me someday.

I get up and start to clean the monstrous mess I made. Every few minutes, I stop to check his vitals. Thankfully, he's still doing well. His heartbeat is stronger than the last time I checked, and his color is coming back. I am beginning to think that I might actually be able to pull off this miracle.

After I give him his next round of medication, I decide to take a break. I grab a sandwich and go sit on the sofa. I turn on the TV, and just as I am throwing a blanket over my legs, my cell phone begins to ring. I reach over and answer it, assuming that it's my dad calling to check in on things.

"Hello?" I wait for a response, but there is nothing. Only silence. The same silence that I've been getting for the past month. I look down and see the same number from the hospital.

"Why do you keep doing this? Why don't you stop being a fucking coward and say something?!" I shout into the phone. I listen hard, hoping to hear some kind of response, but I can hear only the faint rustle of someone's breath. I end the call and toss my phone down on the table. Shit! I drop my head back onto the couch and try to calm my racing heart. I don't know why I don't just give up. I know there is very little chance that they will ever call me back to work, but it is so hard for me to let go of that part of my life. I've wanted to be a doctor for as long as I can remember. I don't want to let them win without a fight.

I turn on the TV and start flipping through the

channels. I finally decide on the cooking channel and am just about to doze off when the phone rings again. I pick up the phone and check to see that it is actually my dad calling before I answer.

"Hey."

"You doing okay over there?" he asks.

"I'm fine," I say, trying to reassure him.

"Any change in your John Doe?"

"Not lately," I say, sitting up on the sofa. I probably need to go check on him again. "He was still asleep the last time I checked on him."

"Call me when he starts to come to. I don't want you to be left alone with this guy when wakes up," he says firmly.

"Okay, but I don't expect that to be any time soon."

"It could be any minute, Ana. Just keep an eye on him."

"I will… promise," I assure him.

"Good. I'll be by first thing in the morning."

"Okay, Daddy. Goodnight." I hang up the phone and throw my blanket to the back of the sofa. I walk down the long hall to the bedroom and stop cold when I notice the set of blue eyes looking back at me. I move a few steps closer, just to be sure that I'm not seeing things. His eyes lock on mine for a brief moment before they flutter shut again. How is he already waking up?

I walk over and sit on the edge of the bed. I run the tips of my fingers across his forehead, brushing his hair to the side. He feels warm to the touch, so I check his temperature. He has a low-grade fever, which concerns me. I'm afraid to leave him before the fever breaks, so after placing a cool washcloth on his head, I pull a chair over to the side of the bed. I prop my feet up on the edge of the mattress and lay my head back on the chair. It isn't the most comfortable way to sleep, but I like being there with him. In some crazy way, it makes me feel safer just having him there beside me.

I spend the next two days watching over him just like that, never leaving his side. There is something peaceful about watching him sleep and listening to the steady rhythm of his breathing. Being in the room with him seems to ease some of the tension I've been feeling.

CHAPTER 5
SHEPPARD

THE SUN COMING through the blinds is so bright that it makes it hard for me to open my eyes, and every fucking muscle in my body feels like it's on fire. I don't want to move, and I sure as hell don't want to open my eyes. Unfortunately, the overwhelming need to take a piss is forcing me to wake up. When I finally make myself open my eyes, I realize that I don't have a clue where I am or how the hell I got here. I glance around the room and can't help but smile as I find my guardian angel asleep beside me.

I thought she was just a dream, but sure enough, here she sits. Her long blonde hair falls loose around her shoulders, framing her angelic face. She has a plaid blanket over her legs, but I can still see the bright red letters that spell out Louisville on her grey t-shirt. She is sound asleep, totally unaware that I am even looking at her. I watch as she takes slow, peaceful breaths and find myself wishing she were sleeping in the bed next to me instead of that stupid chair. She looks so innocent resting there, and her full, pouty lips are just begging to be kissed. I want her to wake up and open her eyes, so I can see if they are green like I remember.

Without thinking, I turn my hips, trying to move my legs off of the bed. My entire body tenses with pain, and I can't stop myself from shouting out, "Fucking hell!"

"Shit!" she screeches as the blanket flies off of her legs, and she races to the doorway. She stops herself before she actually leaves the room and turns back to look at me. Her beautiful eyes widen as they roam over my body. Her face turns pale like she's just seen a ghost. She keeps staring at me like she's trying to decide if I'm really here or just some figment of her imagination.

I try to clear my throat and ask, "You got a name?"

"Ana," she says as a hint of red begins to blush her cheeks. Damn, she's cute.

"This your place, Ana?" I ask.

"Yes."

"Are you the one that did this?" I question as I point to my bandages.

"Yes."

"You a doctor or something?"

"Ummm…" she starts as her eyes drop to the ground. "Kind of."

"You think you could help me to the bathroom?" I ask as I toss the covers off of my body.

Her eyes dart down to my waist and train on my hard cock. I note a spark of curiosity flashing through her eyes as she bites her bottom lip. It's like she's seeing me as a man and not a patient for the first time, and my cock twitches with arousal to her reaction. She quickly turns her head, avoiding eye contact with me. I decide not to embarrass her any more than I already have and try to get out of the bed. Pain soars through me as the bullet wound in my gut twists and pulls, forcing me to stop moving.

"Stop!" she shouts and runs over to the bed. "You're going to hurt yourself!" She places both of her hands on my chest and pushes me back against the pillows. I thought she was beautiful before, but up close, she is fucking amazing. Her green eyes glow with intensity as she urges me to stay put.

"Babe, I gotta take a piss," I tell her boldly.

"Sorry, I had to remove your catheter last night. Give me a minute, and I'll bring you a bedpan." She releases me and starts towards the door.

"Fuck that. I'm not using a damn bedpan… now or ever. I'm getting up now… *with or without* your help," I snap. There is no fucking way I am going to use one of those goddamn things. I try to pull my legs over to the side of the bed, but I don't have the strength to move them more than a few inches.

"Holy hell! Stop acting like a caveman and just be still! You have not one, but *TWO* bullet wounds, and it wasn't exactly easy to keep you from bleeding to death, so I'd *appreciate* it if you wouldn't screw up everything I did to save your life!" she huffs as she throws an empty plastic bottle at me and walks out the door.

I have an overwhelming urge to grab her and throw her over my knee. I think I'd enjoy teaching her a lesson about that sassy mouth of hers, but I can't do anything about it now. I shake my head in frustration as I grab the bottle and use it to take a piss. I don't like anything about this fucking situation. I hate the thought of anyone having to take care of me, especially a woman that looks like her. Why does she have to be so fucking beautiful? I need to get back on my feet and get the hell out of here. I cap off the bottle and try to sit it on the floor, but I can't reach.

Ana storms back into the room and grabs it from my hand. Just before she turns to walk out of the room again, I catch a glimpse of the satisfied smirk that is plastered all over her face. Aw, hell.... She will pay for that shit. A few minutes later, I hear her making all kinds of fucking racket with pots and pans in the front of the house, so I can only assume she's making breakfast. The thought of food turns my stomach. I look down and peel back the bandage on my upper chest. The stitches are clean and precise; nothing like what Doc usually does for us at the clubhouse. This chick really must be some kind of doctor.

She walks back into the room carrying a tray and places it on the dresser. She gives me a look of disapproval as she sees me looking at my wound. I carefully cover it back up and stare at the tray of food.

"I'm not hungry," I tell her.

"Maybe not, but you really need to eat something," she says as she walks over to me. She gently places the palm of her hand on my forehead and looks at me with genuine concern. My eyes lock on hers as she slowly lowers her hand to my wrist to check my pulse. Her eyebrows crinkle together as she tries to focus on my heartbeat. "What about some toast?" she asks.

"No."

"Cereal?"

"No."

"Umm… bacon and eggs?"

"Look, I appreciate it, but I'm just not hungry," I explain.

"You haven't had any real food in days, and these are strong antibiotics. They're going to make you feel worse if you don't have something on your stomach," she warns.

"Just give me the damn medicine, and I'll eat something later," I tell her.

"*Okay*, but no complaining when your stomach starts cramping, and you end up feeling worse," she says scornfully.

"Fine, do you have any crackers?" I ask.

"Sure do," she replies as she grabs the sleeve of crackers from the tray and tosses them onto the bed. Then, she takes a bottle of water off of the tray and places it on the bedside table. "I'll be back in a few minutes with your medicine. Do you need anything else?"

"Some clothes, unless you like having me like *this*," I say as I lift the sheet just enough to make my point. I smile as I watch her cheeks turn a dark shade of pink.

"My father… he's… uh… bringing you some things when he comes this morning," she stammers.

I nod. At that moment, I realize I have no idea what

the hell is really going on here. I don't even know where I am. Why didn't she just take me to the hospital or call an ambulance? I need to pull my head out of my ass and find out what is going on. I look around the room, searching for any information about the woman that has just saved my life. I don't see anything suspicious. From the looks of the pictures around the room, she isn't involved with anyone. I wonder why a girl like her isn't already married with two point five kids. From what I can tell, she lives out here alone, and something about that pisses me off. She had no business bringing some stranger into her home like this without having someone here to help her.

I am lost in my thoughts when I catch sight of her standing in the doorway, staring at me. "You ready?" she asks.

"Guess so," I tell her. She walks over to the side of the bed and holds out her hand with the pills resting in her palm.

I take them from her and use the bottle of water to choke them down. "Thanks."

"You want to tell me what happened?" she asks. "Is someone going to be coming after you?"

"It's a long story, but you don't have to worry about that. Everyone thinks I'm dead."

"Who shot you? Why would someone want to hurt you?"

"Doesn't matter," I tell her.

"I think I have a right to know," she snaps. "Remember, I'm the one that just dragged you out of that freezing lake and saved your life."

"Look, Ana. I appreciate everything you've done, but I'm not getting into all that with you right now."

"What about your family or friends? Do they think you're dead?"

"No idea," I lie, knowing there is no way they think I survived.

"I just saved your life. How can you not tell me?"

"It's for your own safety," I tell her.

"Whatever," she says, rolling her eyes spitefully. Yeah, there is no doubt that I'll be taking this girl over my knee.

"How long do you think it'll be before I'm back on my feet?"

"Honestly, I'm shocked that you're even alive. The water in the lake must have been cold enough to slow your metabolism down and keep you from bleeding to death. You're very lucky," she explains.

"How long?" I ask again.

"Couple of weeks, maybe three," she responds.

"Hell no," I bark. "There's no way I'm going to be laid up here for two or three fucking weeks."

"Why don't you just save your little tantrum for another day? I have too much to deal with right now, and you're acting like…." She suddenly stops when her phone begins to ring in her back pocket. A strange look crosses her face just before her eyes drop to the floor. She slowly reaches for her phone and looks at the screen, seeming reluctant to answer it.

She cautiously lifts the phone to her ear and whispers, "Hello?" It's like a totally different person is standing here in front of me, and I don't like it. "Hello?" she says again, a little louder this time. She stands there silent for a few brief moments before she lets out a deep sigh and hangs up the phone.

"Damn it," she mutters in a defeated voice. She looks over to me and says, "I'm going to go make some coffee. Do you need anything?"

"What was that all about?" I ask.

"It's nothing…." she replies with a shake of her head. Something about the way she'd looked in that moment got to me, though. I want to know what is going on, but I know this isn't the time to push her. Something is drawing me to her. It makes me want to know everything there is to know about her.

"My name is Dillon." I have no idea what possesses me to tell her my real name, but I like the way her expression changes as I say it.

"Dillon?" she asks as her lips curve into a beautiful smile. "You look like a Dillon. It suits you."

"So, Ana… when is your dad coming with those clothes?" I ask.

"He should be here any minute. I should warn you, though," she adds, tucking her hair behind her ear. "He wasn't exactly happy about me bringing you here. He's going to ask a lot of questions."

"If he's anything like you, I'm sure he will," I said with a laugh.

"You could always pretend to still be sleeping. It might be easier."

"Not doing that," I snap. "I can handle your dad."

"Don't say I didn't warn ya," she says, shrugging. She jumps when the doorbell rings. "That's him. I'll be back in a little bit."

I watch the curve of her ass as she walks out of the room. Damn. Yeah, there is definitely something about this woman that captivates me. There are secrets locked away behind those beautiful green eyes, and I want to know all of them. A part of me knows I won't like it, but that won't stop me from finding out what she's hiding.

CHAPTER 6

ANA

THEY'VE BEEN BACK there for over an hour, and Dad won't even let me come into the room. I have no idea what they are talking about, and it's driving me nuts. Dad just told me he wanted to get things sorted, and that it would be better if he did it alone. I don't like it, but I know he's right. I'm sure Dillon feels better talking to my dad without me listening in anyways.

I jump when the door to my bedroom opens, and my dad comes walking out. His eyes are focused on me as he makes his way down the long hallway. "Well?" I ask anxiously.

"If he's telling the truth, then I think we did the right thing bringing him here," he responds. "He seems like a very decent young man."

"That's good news then, right?"

"Yeah, but you need to be smart about this, Ana. It's going to take some time for him to heal, so I made some ground rules for while he's here," he explains.

"What kind of rules?" I ask.

"I let him know what my expectations are. He has a

life waiting for him, so as soon as he gets back on his feet, he needs to go home."

"That's the plan, Daddy. I never expected him to stay."

"Don't go falling for this guy. He's already showing an interest in you… asking a lot of questions and trying to find out what's going on with you."

"I have no interest in starting anything up with him," I say, trying to sound like I mean it. "It's not like he's my type anyway."

"You don't have a type yet, and I don't want you to get hurt," he warns. That's like telling me to go jump in the sack with the guy right now. I've never been very good with people telling me not to do something, especially my dad.

"And Steven called. Said he's been trying to reach you, but you haven't answered his calls," Dad says with a questioning look. "Just a heads up… he's coming by this afternoon to check on you."

"Why didn't you just make something up? Tell him I have the flu or I'm on my period or something," I groan.

"He knows something is going on, so you might as well figure out what you're going to tell him about your guest."

"His name is Dillon, and there's nothing to tell. He won't even tell me anything!" I shout.

"Well, either way, Steven's coming. You decide what you want to tell him," he barks as he walks towards the door. "I have to run into town. Call me if you need anything."

He shuts the door before I have a chance to say anything more. Damn. I am totally screwed. Steven is going to have a meltdown when he finds out about all this. I actually feel a little bad about it. He's been so supportive over the past few months, and I know this is going to push him over the edge. I actually consider not telling him, but he can always tell when I'm keeping things from him. He knows me better than anyone, so there's no point in even trying to hide this.

I make Dillon a bowl of chicken soup and crackers for lunch. He is exhausted and falls asleep before he even finishes eating. I'm busy cleaning up his dishes when Steven knocks on the door. He doesn't wait for me to answer. Instead, he uses his key and walks right in.

"What's going on with you, Ana? I've been calling you for days, and you won't answer your damn phone," Steven says with a disgruntled look on his face. The dark burgundy shirt that he's wearing only makes him look even angrier, and I find it hard to look him in the eye.

"I've been... umm... really busy, Steven. Dad has been helping me with something, and... it's been a little hectic," I stutter.

"What kind of something, and why haven't you answered the phone?" he asks. "Just tell me what the hell is going on."

"It's nothing, Steven. Really. Nothing to worry about. I'm sorry I didn't answer my phone."

"Have you been getting those calls again?" he asks.

"Well, they never really stopped...." I confess.

"Wait... I thought you said they were getting better!"

he snaps.

"I lied."

"Fuck! Why the hell haven't you told me?" he shouts as he begins pacing around the room. He runs his fingers through his hair, and his eyes narrow on mine. "You can't keep going on like this, Ana. We have to do something."

"We've already tried everything. There's nothing else we can do. I don't want you to keep worrying about all this. It's not your problem," I explain.

"I can't believe you just said that. Fucking hell, Ana," he says angrily as he sits down on one of my kitchen stools. "I want to be there for you, but you have to let me know what's going on."

"I'm sorry. You're right. I shouldn't have kept that from you," I mutter as I look down at the floor.

"What else haven't you told me?" he asks.

My insides twist into a ball of nerves as I say, "Well…."

"What?" he asks, crossing his arms over his chest.

I sit down next to him and try my best to explain everything that has happened over the past few days. Several times he tries to lift himself off of the stool to go see for himself what I've gotten myself into, but I'm able to hold him off until I finish telling him everything.

"You should've called me! I could have taken him to the hospital outside of town or…." he starts.

"He wouldn't have survived that long. He was barely alive when I found him. I honestly didn't have a choice," I explain.

He gets up from his stool and storms down the hallway into my bedroom. Dillon's eyes fly open as Steven enters the room. He looks over to me with a questioning look.

"Um, Dillon, this is Steven. He's... a really good friend of mine," I try to explain. I look over to Steven and watch as he rolls his eyes.

Dillon nods, but neither of them speaks. They just stare at each other, speaking volumes with their silence. I watch as Steven's eyes skirt over the tattoos on Dillon's arms. Thankfully, he'd put on the t-shirt and pajama pants that my father had brought earlier, but that doesn't do much for hiding the brightly colored ink that covers his body. I look back over to Dillon. He seems amused by Steven's reaction, and it's only making matters worse. I need to break the tension building in the room, but I'm not sure what to say.

"Uh... Steven, we should let Dillon get some rest." Steven glares at me as he turns and heads out of my bedroom.

"What are you thinking?" he barks as he walks down the hallway and into the kitchen. He stops when he reaches my front door and drops his head. He stays that way for several seconds before he turns back to me and says, "I've really tried to be there for you, Ana, but this is just too much."

"You're my best friend, Steven. I appreciate everything you've done for me, but I can take care of myself. I can handle this," I say, trying to ease some of the tension between us.

"I've loved you since the night I saw you searching for your cat in the backyard wearing nothing but your t-shirt and knickers. There's nothing in this world I wouldn't do for you," he says in a low voice, almost a whisper. He is lost in his thoughts for a moment before he continues, "What happens when this guy ends up hurting you?"

"He won't... I won't let that happen," I promise.

He lets out a deep sigh and walks out of the house. I consider going after him, but I know it is better to give him some time. I know he loves me and wants the best for me, but he has to learn to let me make my own choices... whether they're right or wrong.

CHAPTER 7

SHEPPARD

THE CONVERSATION I had with Ana's father keeps replaying over and over in my head. Everything he said made sense, but I'm not sure I can follow through. News of the shooting at Calvert City had made the newspapers, and it didn't take much for him to figure out that I was involved. Even after I explained what I could, he was still concerned. He was worried that I might bring trouble for Ana, so he asked me not to contact anyone while I'm here.

"She's all I've got. I'll do anything to protect her," he'd said as tears filled his eyes. It gutted me, and I knew then that I had to agree to his request. I couldn't guarantee that our troubles with the Black Diamonds were over, so I agreed not to contact my brothers. I couldn't risk putting her in danger after everything she'd done to save my life. Besides, I've decided that I like the thought of being here with her until I get back on my feet. I can't think of any place I'd rather be.

"Ana!" I call out. I've been lying in this bed for hours, and now I have to go to the bathroom. I am in desperate need of a hot shower, and I'm dying to get the hell out of this bed. I know she'll give me hell about it, but I can't stand it any longer. "Ana!"

"I'm coming," she shouts from the room beside me. I can hear her knocking around, and I wonder what the hell she's doing.

"Ana!" I demand once again.

"HOLD ON! I said I'm coming!" she shouts as she rushes into the room. Her hair is wet and falling all around her shoulders. She's forgotten to fasten a few buttons on her pale blue shirt, and my eyes are drawn to the hint of cleavage it reveals. "What?"

I clear my throat before I say, "Need help getting out of this bed. I need to go to the bathroom and want to take a shower."

"Can you give me a few minutes? I need to get things set up to make it easier for you," she explains.

"You aren't going to fight me on this?" I ask her.

"I don't see the point. You're just going to keep pestering me until you get your way. Just let me make sure you don't hurt yourself while you do it," she sighs.

"I can go along with that," I reply.

"I'll be right back." She leaves the room but quickly returns with a tall chair. I hear her bang it into the wall as she drags it into the bathroom. She leaves the room again, only to return with plastic wrap and new bandages.

"Okay, I have to make sure you don't get the stitches wet," she states as she drops everything on the bed beside me. "Do you need help taking off your shirt?"

"Yes."

Her warm fingers brush against the sides of my waist as she reaches for the hem of my shirt. She slowly eases the shirt off of my body, trying her best not to hurt me. Once she tosses the shirt to the end of the bed, she begins securing the clear plastic wrap over my bandages.

When she's done, she asks, "You ready?"

I nod and drag my legs to the side of the bed. I cringe when the pain wrenches through my gut, but I don't let it stop me. I continue to inch my way over to the edge of the bed, and once I get there, I look over to Ana. She walks over to me and sits down, reaching for my arm. She slowly brings it up to her shoulder, and leans into my side, taking some of the burden of my weight. I let out a deep breath as we slowly stand together. She brings her other arm around my waist to help guide me into the bathroom.

When we finally make it to the sink, I grab the counter and use it as support. I look over at her and smile with approval. I am impressed. I'd doubted that a woman her size could help get me out of that bed, but she proved me wrong.

Her cheeks become bright red when she looks down at my boxers and asks, "Umm… do you need any help with those?" I mean, the woman's basically a doctor. I know she's seen naked men before, so I can only assume her reaction is for me. That thought brings a smile to my face.

"I got it," I tell her with a smirk.

"I'll give you a few minutes before I come back to help you get in the shower," she tells me as she backs out of the door.

Getting those damn boxers off hurts like a bitch, but it's worth it to finally use the toilet like a normal human being. After a few seconds, Ana comes back into the bathroom. Without saying a word, she reaches into the shower and turns on the water, holding her hand under the faucet until it's warm enough.

"Ready?" she asks as she awkwardly stares at my chest. I know she's trying her best not to look at my dick, but that's going to be damn near impossible when she helps me get in that shower.

"Yeah," I tell her. I take a few steps towards her before my knees give out, causing me to drop down on top of her. She wraps her arms around my waist, supporting me until I get my footing.

"You okay?"

"I'm fine. Just lost my balance."

"I'm going to step in with you and help you get into the chair," she explains as she leads us over to the shower door. "When you're ready, I'll leave you to it."

I nod and try to concentrate on making it to that damn chair without falling on my ass like a fucking idiot. I'm beginning to regret this whole plan of mine. Every inch of my body is on fire, and I don't know if I will have the strength to get back to the damn bed. Ana gently lowers me into the chair. She holds me close to her until she knows I'm okay. I immediately miss her touch when she releases me, and I fight the urge to pull her back into my arms. She stands in front of me with her wet shirt clinging to her breasts, showing off her perfect tits. Even in a haze of pain, my cock jumps to life when I realize that she isn't wearing a bra. Amazingly, she is totally unaware of the effect that she's having on me as she smiles bashfully and steps out of the shower.

"I'll be right back. Just holler if you need me," she whispers.

I close my eyes and let the warm water run down my body, relieving some of the tension that was building in my aching muscles. By the time I finish taking my shower, the entire room is clouded with steam. I shut off the water and reach for the towel Ana had left on the rail and place it over my waist. "Ana?" I call.

"Coming," she yells. She quickly opens the door and heads over to me. A small smile spreads across her face when she notices the towel I placed across my lap. "Ready?" she asks as she grabs an extra towel from the cabinet and places it around my shoulders.

Without answering, I place my hands on her shoulders, using them to help pull myself up from the chair. She eases me out of the shower, being careful not to pull any of my stitches. After I tighten the towel around my waist, we slowly make our way back over to the bed. Each step is filled with excruciating pain, but I'm determined to get back to that damn bed without falling. I need to start building my strength so I won't have to rely on her so much next time. When we reach the bed, she takes the towel from my shoulders and uses it to dry me off.

"Do you want a fresh shirt?" she asks.

"Not yet," I tell her as I slowly lower myself to the

edge of the bed. Once I'm sitting, she innocently kneels down between my legs so she can begin removing the bandages. I try not to let my mind go where it wants to go, but fuck it's hard. When she reaches up to remove the first bandage, her breasts press up against me, begging me to reach out and touch them. Fuck. She has to be messing with me. I shake my head, trying to clear my thoughts. I look down and watch as she peels back the first bandage. I am relieved to see that I didn't cause any damage to the stitches during my shower. "They still looking okay?" I ask.

"Yes, but you're going to need some fresh dressings. If you lay back, I'll change them for you." She puts her hands behind my shoulders, helping me lean back onto the pillows, and then she helps bring my legs to the center of the bed.

She leans over me and begins applying the new bandages on my chest. I am totally mesmerized as I watch her lay each piece of gauze carefully on my chest. A few loose strands of hair fall in her face, and I gently tuck them back behind her ear. Touching her sends a jolt of need through me. Her breathing instantly becomes irregular and her hands tremble as I continue to watch her every move. When she starts to bite her bottom lip, I can't take it anymore.

I reach up, taking her face in my hands, and gently pull her over to me. Something inside of me ignites the minute her lips touch mine. A fire is set deep inside me, and I know in that instant that I'll never get enough of her. A light moan escapes her as my tongue brushes against her bottom lip, fueling my need for more. I lower my hands to her neck and pull her closer, needing to feel her body against mine. I want her… all of her. I ignore the gnawing pain in my side as I take my time claiming her mouth with my tongue… warm and wet. Fuck. I'd give anything if I could spend the night exploring her perfect mouth. Even with the exhaustion taking over me, I have to have more of her. I want to know what it feels like to be inside her, know every fucking inch of that perfect little body of hers. I am totally lost in her touch when she begins to pull away from me. Fuck, I don't want to let her go… but she's leaving me no choice. She places her hands on my chest and frees herself from my embrace. I growl with disapproval and reluctantly let her go.

"I don't think…." she starts.

"Don't," I interrupt.

"What?"

"You know what," I say, pulling her back over to me. She doesn't protest as she gently lays her head on my shoulder. I put my arm behind her as she curls up next to me and waits quietly for me to fall asleep.

When I wake up, she's gone. I wish I could say that the kiss was the start of something between us… that since she'd had a taste of me, she only wants more. Unfortunately, that isn't the case.

Over the next couple of days, she is cold and distant, playing the part of a doctor perfectly. I am fed up with it, though, and tonight that shit is going to end.

CHAPTER 8

ANA

WHY THE HELL did he have to go and kiss me like that? The spark that shot through me when his lips touched mine went straight to my soul. It's the only thing I've been able to think about, and I can't seem to wrap my head around it. I've never felt like that before, and since it happened, I've been trying my best to avoid him. I go in to give him his meds and check his vitals, but I leave before he really has a chance to talk to me. I feel so silly acting like this, but I can't stop myself. I don't know how to act when he's sitting there with that sexy smirk on his face. It's like he's enjoying the effect that he's having on me. I try my best not to look at him, but I can feel the heat of his stare scorching my skin when I walk in and out of the room.

I'm being ridiculous. It was just a kiss, and I'm acting like a freaking idiot. I need to get my shit together and help him get back on his feet. A man like him isn't going to want to wait around here much longer. The thought of him leaving makes my heart drop deep into my chest, but I know it's only a matter of time before he'll be ready to get back to his life. I've got to stop acting like a fool and do whatever it takes to get him ready to go home.

I gather up his lunch and head down the hall. His back is propped up on several pillows, and he's watching TV. As I glance over to him, my eyes take on a life of their own and slowly roam over his body. He's all rugged with his three-day-old beard and tousled hair. Damn. He looks so good sitting there wearing those plaid sleep pants and that old faded t-shirt. When I finally stop ogling and look him in the eye, the TV goes mute. The expression on his face lets me know that he has something on his mind, but I'm not sure I'm ready to hear what he has to say.

Trying to calm the nervousness that I feel growing in my stomach, I turn to him and say, "We're under a winter storm warning, so I'm going to need to get some groceries before it gets here. Is there anything you want me to get while I'm out?"

"How about a movie or something?"

"I can do that. What kind of movies do you like?" I ask.

"Just pick something you'd like to watch. I don't care what it is. I'm up for anything," he says with a smile.

My heart begins to beat faster as I realize he wants to watch the movie with me. "Hmm… okay. I'll be back in a couple of hours," I tell him as I head towards the door.

"Ana?" he calls.

I turn back to him and say, "Yeah?"

"Grab some popcorn or something, too."

I smile at him before I head out the door. When I get

into town, I realize that everyone must have had the same idea I did. I can barely even find a parking place, and the store is crazy crowded. Everyone is loading up their shopping carts like they're preparing for the apocalypse, and by the time I make it down the first aisle, I'm ready to get the hell out of there. I grab a few of the basics like bread and milk, and then I go hunt for the popcorn. Once I have everything we'll need for the next few days, I get in the longest line in history. Everyone looks disgruntled and eager to get out of there. Of course, I pick the line that has the slowest cashier, but I do my best to be patient. After forty-five minutes of just plain torture, I finally make my way out of the store.

Thankfully, the movie store isn't very crowded. I take my time roaming up and down the rows of movies trying to find something I think he will actually like. I have no idea, so I just grab a bunch of the new releases, hoping that one of them will spark some interest. After picking out a few extra snacks, I check out and head home.

On the way, I notice a black sports car following close behind me as I turn off on the old country road that leads to my house. At first, I don't think much about it, but then they take every turn I make. Panic begins to set in when the car follows me onto my last turn, trailing just inches away from my bumper. No one really ever comes down this road, so I know something isn't right. I start to drive a little faster, hoping to get rid of them, but they won't budge. I don't want them to follow me home, so I take the back road to my dad's. I panic as I notice that Dad's truck isn't in the driveway, but thankfully they don't follow me to his house. My heart races as I peer out my window, searching for the person who was following me. It's hard to see anything with all the trees blocking my view, so I wait there long enough to make sure they are really gone. When I feel certain I'm alone, my nerves finally begin to settle. I ease my car into reverse and head back home, constantly checking my rear view mirror to make sure they don't come back.

My hands are still trembling as I unload the car, but as soon as I walk into my house, everything seems okay. I know it's crazy, but having Dillon there makes me feel safer. It doesn't really make any sense. The man can hardly get out of the bed without help, but his presence really does set my mind at ease.

I go back to check on him, and he's hobbling out of the bathroom when I walk in. I go over and offer him my shoulder. He reluctantly takes it and says, "I could've made it on my own."

"Stubborn," I say, raising my eyebrow.

"I like to think I'm determined."

"No… you're just stubborn," I tell him with a laugh. I help him to edge of the bed and say, "I thought I'd make us some spaghetti for dinner."

"Did you get a movie?" he asks.

"I got several. I wasn't sure what you'd like."

"I told you to pick one you'd like," he tells me as he eases back onto the bed.

"I like anything," I say with a shrug. "I'm going to make dinner. Do you need anything?"

"Can I help?" he asks. I want to laugh, but I can tell

by his expression that he's being serious.

"Getting a little cabin fever?" I ask.

"You have no fucking idea."

"How about trying to move to the sofa for a little while? The change of scenery might help," I offer.

"It's worth a shot. I'm about to lose my mind in here."

Once he's settled on the sofa, I go into the kitchen and start dinner. I'm almost done making the salad when my phone rings. I look down at the screen, and my skin crawls with anger. I am completely fed up with this bullshit. I've given up all hope that someone from the hospital will call to say that my suspension has been lifted. I know who is calling, so I answer, determined to end this once and for all.

"Hello!" I roar into the phone. After a few seconds of silence I say, "Hello, asshole. Why do you keep wasting my time? Stop being a damn coward and say something!" Still no response. "I'm done with this! If you want me, come and get me!" I screech as I take my phone and throw it across the room. I watch with great satisfaction as it hits the wall and shatters.

"What the hell was that?" Dillon shouts from across the room. Shit! I was totally caught up in the moment and forgot he was even there. My eyes shoot over to him, and I'm surprised by the look of anger on his face.

"It's nothing," I say nonchalantly, hoping that he won't make a big deal out of it.

"*That*," he says as he points to the scattered mess that used to be my phone, "isn't nothing."

"It's not a big deal. Just don't worry about it," I say as I turn back to the salad.

"Ana," he growls. I look over to him and he says, "Stop. I want to know what the hell is going on. It's obvious that something is up with you. Now, I want to know what the hell it is."

His stare is intense, letting me know that he has no intention of letting this go. I want to tell him everything, but I just don't see the point. There is nothing that he can do. "Really, Dillon. It's okay. You don't…." I start.

"Now, Ana."

I stare at him, trying to understand why he even cares. From the first moment I laid eyes on him, I knew he wasn't like any man I'd ever met. I felt so drawn to him on the one hand, but I didn't even know how to act around him on the other. Hell, most of the time I want to clock him in the head, but then there are times that I have to fight the urge to kiss him. My feelings for him are so strong and overwhelming; it is beyond frustrating. I consider telling him to go to hell, but there is a nagging part of me that wants him to know what's going on. I need him to know.

"It's a long story," I try to explain.

"I'm not going anywhere. Come over here and tell me what's going on."

I turn the oven off, walk into the living room, and sit in the recliner next to him. I slowly drag my fingers across my eyes and temples as I try to decide where to start.

"Ana," he demands.

"Okay," I say sarcastically. "I'll tell you everything, even though you won't tell me *anything*.... But it isn't going to help."

He sits patiently and listens as I tell him everything that happened with my suspension, and everything that has been happening since. There were several times that he looked confused, like he was trying to piece it all together. It was a lot to take in.

He waits until I've told him everything before he asks, "Tell me more about Jason. What do you know about him?"

"He's one of those rich kid brats that doesn't like it when things don't go his way. I didn't realize how bad things really were until I found out his father actually owns the hospital. There's no way I'm ever going to get out of this mess," I explain.

"What about those patients you questioned him about? What was the deal with them?" he asks.

"There were some discrepancies in their charts... wrong medications, and they were running unnecessary tests on some of the patients."

"What happened to them?"

"I don't know. I was suspended later that afternoon, so I wasn't able to find out."

"Do you remember their names?"

"Yeah, I wrote them down when I noticed the problems," I tell him. It's strange how just talking about this with him is giving me some sense of hope, like maybe there is something he can do to help me. I know it's stupid of me to think that he would even want to help, but I actually feel like there's a chance for the first time in months.

"Good. I want to know everything that you have on Jason and his family and those patients at the hospital. If there is anything else you can think of, I want to know that, too."

"Why?" I ask.

"Just get it for me, okay?"

"Okay," I reply. We sit there quietly for a few brief moments just staring at each other. I don't know what it is about this man, but I feel such a connection to him. I long to be closer to him. I want to go over to that sofa and just press my lips against his, but I'm frozen in my seat… unable to even speak.

"So, how about that spaghetti? I'm starving," he asks with a smile.

I don't answer. I just get up and go into the kitchen to get everything ready. Just as I am about to take him his dinner, I notice that the snow is beginning to fall. I can hear the light taps of sleet hit the windowpane, and I begin to wonder if it's going to be as bad as everyone says it's going to be. Even though it's been nice, this weather is pretty typical for this time of year. For some reason, we seem to get our worst winter weather in February and March. Lately, we've gotten more ice storms than actual snow, and I'm not a fan of ice storms.

We talk all through dinner, and he finally shares a little about his life back in Paris. His face lights up when he tells me about his club and his brothers. Each one of them seems to hold a special place in his heart, making me want to meet them for myself. I'd heard about motorcycle clubs like his, but I'd never known anyone that was actually a member. I'd always been a little curious about them, wondering if they were filled with dangerous men just looking for trouble. Even the shows on TV made them out to be villains, but hearing him talk about it made me realize how wrong I had been about them. These clubs brought people together and created families that cared a great deal about one another. I really want to go to Tennessee and meet them for myself, but I know it is doubtful that will ever happen. Once he's back on his feet, Dillon will be gone, and I'll probably never see him again.

"I'll need to get in touch with them soon. Let them know I'm okay," he explains.

"Well, I'm sure they'll be excited to hear that you're okay," I tell him, trying not to sound too disappointed. I look towards the window, unable to face him. I had always known he was only going to be here until he was mobile, but I hated the thought of him leaving so soon.

"Which movie do you want to watch?" I'm relieved that he's trying to change the subject. I'm not ready to deal with him going just yet.

"I'm up for anything. You pick," I tell him, handing him the stack of movies.

Without even looking, he grabs one of the movies and hands it to me. "Let's watch this one."

I look down at the title and smile. He picked one of the scary movies I'd wanted to see for months. I usually don't watch them, because I hate being in the house alone after seeing one. I thought I might try it tonight since he is here, though. I really doubt that he'll even like it, but I decide not to try and talk him out of it. I get up and put the movie in the DVD player. After turning out a few of the lights, I head back towards the recliner.

"No… sit over here with me," he says, moving his legs over to make room for me.

I don't resist, mainly because I don't want to. I'm thrilled at the idea of being close, even if it is just for a little while. He pulls at the blanket, offering me enough to cover my legs. Once I get settled, I look back over to him. With just the glow of the television screen, I can see that his blue eyes are focused on me, and my heart pounds in my chest. My body tingles everywhere. I want to reach out and feel him, to know the touch of his skin against mine. Resisting the immense temptation, I look back over to the TV. After a few minutes, the creepy music begins to play, and the main character is sitting in a dark house seemingly unaware of the danger lurking behind the closed door.

"What is it with women and scary movies?" he asks.

"Hey, I gave you the chance to pick. Who knows? You might like it," I tease. "Either way, it's too late now."

"Oh, is that right?" he snickers. "We'll see how you feel about scary movies when the lights go out from the storm."

"Shit," I mutter under my breath. "I hadn't really thought about that." I love my little house, but it gives me the freaking creeps when the lights go out. It's completely back in the woods, and I feel so secluded when I'm out here alone.

"Don't worry, I'll protect you from all the things that go bump in the night," he says, laughing out loud.

"Somehow, that doesn't exactly make me feel better. You can barely make it across the room without help," I tell him playfully.

"Hey, I'm doing better. I could totally kick some ghost's ass if I needed to," he says confidently.

"Right, I'm sure you can," I mock.

"Don't you doubt it for a minute," he says with a smile.

"Just so you know, if something does come after us, I'm not one of those girls that will wait for you, pulling you along as the bad guys come after us… and I really doubt that I'd come back to help even when the coast was clear. Because let's face it… the coast is *never* clear. I would just run without looking back, and I wouldn't give it a second thought."

"Now, that's just mean. I would come back for you," he says, sounding defensive. I can't hold back my laughter. He seems so sincere that I almost tell him I'm kidding, but that would take the fun out of it. I know there is no way I'd ever be able to leave him behind. I'd already proven that.

"Ahh… that's sweet. Still not coming back for you, though," I snicker. I am now laughing so hard my stomach hurts.

"Really? *Really*?"

"There's no reason for both of us to die," I try to tell

him.

"That's fucked up. I can't believe you just said that!"

"I'm kidding, Dillon. I wouldn't let the Boogie Man get you!"

"Nah, it's too late now," he says, shaking his head in disbelief. "And I thought you were sweet."

"Sweet? No, I am definitely not sweet," I snort.

"You're all kinds of sweet, Ana. I like it." The minute the words come out of his mouth, the room turns quiet. I focus my attention back to the movie, not knowing what to say to him. I want to tell him that I like him, too, but I worry that I'm reading too much into things. He's just being nice. Of course he thinks I'm sweet, I just saved his life.

I am relieved that the movie is just scary enough to distract us both from the awkward tension of our earlier conversation. Every time it starts to get frightening, I inch a little closer to him. By the time the movie is over, I am practically lying on top of him. The credits start to scroll across the screen, so I get up and look out the window. It's really coming down. The trees and back porch are totally covered in ice. It's beautiful, but I worry that it won't be long before the power goes out.

"Wanna watch another one?" I ask, thinking we might as well make the best of it while we still can.

"You got another scary one?" he asks.

"I think so. Why?"

"Play it," he tells me. I'm putting the new movie in when I hear my sofa pillows hit the floor. I look back, and Dillon is tossing them all to the ground.

"Whatcha doing?"

"Making room for you," he says, like it isn't a big deal at all. He says it like we've done this kind of thing a thousand times. His words are nonchalant, but they're laced with expectations. He wants me to lay down with him while we watch the movie. Holy crap! How the hell did this just happen?

CHAPTER 9

SHEPPARD

THIS GIRL IS totally fucking with my head. Her warm body is pressed against mine as we lay here watching another one of these damn scary movies, and I can't get enough of her. She's absolutely the most beautiful creature I've ever seen, and she's so close that I can feel her heart beat against my chest. My hands tremble with need, wanting to touch her…to feel her soft skin. I want to let my fingers roam over the curves of her body, exploring every inch of her. She's almost asleep, and I hate that the movie is almost over. I don't want her to move. I want to keep her here next to me, but when the lights start to flicker, I know we need to start a fire. The temperature is dropping, and we'll need something to keep us warm.

"Where do you keep your firewood?" I ask her.

She curls her hands up and semi yawns as she rubs her eyes, trying to wake herself up before she says, "In the garage. I'll go get some."

"I'll get it. Just need to know where it is."

"Umm, no. I'll get it. I don't want you pulling your

stitches. It'll just take a minute. I'll be right back," she said, throwing the covers off her legs. I hate that she's fucking right. I'm starting to feel a lot better, but I'm not up to manual stuff just yet. The stitches are still fairly fresh, and I don't need to take any chances on tearing them. I need a few more days, but I'm getting closer. She clambers back into the room, and her arms are full of lumber.

"Is this the only fireplace?" I ask.

"Yeah. If we lose power, we'll have to sleep in here," she speaks softly, as she slowly turns her head away from me. I have to fight back my smile as I watch her face turn bright red from embarrassment. So fucking cute!

"If you wanted to sleep with me, all you had to do was ask," I tell her playfully and laugh, knowing she's pouting.

She looks straight at me, trying to seem angry, which she doesn't quite manage, then rolls her eyes. "Whatever," she says sarcastically. "I'll be right back. Try to *behave*."

While she goes back to the garage for a second load of wood, I ease myself off the sofa and try to find some paper to get a fire going. I grab some of the newspapers she's stashed in the corner, and then I hunt for a lighter. I find one on the carved stone mantelpiece. I twist the paper really tight and grab a handful of the firewood she fetched and toss it into the hearth. Then, I start flicking the small wheel on the cheap lighter, taking at least ten tries to get a flame. I finally get it to work and light the fire. I look down with pride as I see the small flames growing in the fireplace. She walks back in carrying two small logs and sees what I've done. I get a very disapproving look, but I can tell she doesn't mean it.

"I told you to behave," she says flippantly.

"Knock it off. Give me those," I tell her as I take the logs and put them in the fireplace.

She goes back for more wood saying, "I might as well fill up the wood basket just in case we need it."

I nod and watch her walk out of the room, and then I make my way back over to the sofa. I cringe in pain when I lie back. I strained my wounds more than I should've, but I'll do my best to hide it. There's no way that I'm going to let Ana find out that I hurt myself and give her the satisfaction of being right.

Once the basket is stocked, giving us plenty of logs for the night, she glances at me lying on the sofa. She looks beautiful standing there by the open flame of the fire. The room is now warm with the unmistakable smell of burning logs. Just by looking at me, she has to know that I'm exhausted. I could drop off to sleep right now, and my body would be completely content. I close my eyes slowly a couple of times as I fight to stay awake. I finally manage to say, "You really are an angel," as my eyes close again.

She walks past me and gently strokes my hair. I'm just about asleep when I hear her banging around in the bedroom. I'm immediately pissed off as it dawns on me that she's trying to move that damn mattress by herself. I get off the sofa and head down the hall.

"I can do this. Really! It's not that heavy. Just let me

do it," she pleads.

I ignore her and help her lift it off the bed. The lights blink on and off as we push it down the hallway. My wounds throb in pain, but I do my best to keep it from her. I'd rather not hear her tell me she was right. She throws some blankets and pillows on the mattress, while I light some candles.

As I'm putting another log on the dwindling fire, she says, "You've done enough. Please lay down while I go lock up for the night."

I nod, knowing she is right and carefully lower myself down on the makeshift bed. My aching muscles immediately feel better once I lie down and make myself comfortable. As the throbbing pain slowly subsides, I smile to myself, knowing that Ana is going to be sleeping in this bed with me tonight. She is still wandering around the house locking up when the power finally goes off, plunging the place into darkness.

"All secure," she tells me as she walks back into the room. I look up and notice she's changed into some black leggings and an oversized Kentucky t-shirt. She stands there for a moment, keys still in her hand. She looks around, taking in the splendor of the room, which is now only partially illuminated by the flickering yellow and blue tipped flames of the fire. She is clearly on edge as she walks to the stone mantel. The keys fall from her hand, and she turns back to me. "Well, this is nice and warm," she says bashfully. There's indecision lurking within her eyes as she looks at me. I want her. I want all of her. I feel like just blurting it out, telling her exactly how I feel, but I'm willing to wait until she's ready.

The howling wind and the sound of the ice hitting the windows break the silence of the room as she slowly kneels down on the edge of the mattress. A warm feeling of satisfaction rolls over me as she curls up in the spot next to me. I protectively pull the blankets over us and do my best to resist the urge to grab her and pull her body against mine. I want to lay here and just enjoy having her close to me, but I can barely keep my eyes open. When I can't fight it any longer, I let myself fall asleep.

I wake several times throughout the night from the sounds of nearby trees crashing to the ground. The daunting weight of the falling ice is just too much for them. I'm tempted to get up to see how bad things are getting, but I don't want to move. The fire is dying down to only glowing embers, and Ana is curled up close to me, pressing her ass into my groin. I lay my head down on the pillow just inches from hers and inhale deeply, taking in the scent of her hair. I slip my arm around her waist as she squirms closer to me. I'm almost relieved that I'm too tired to think; otherwise I'd have one hell of a hard on. I close my eyes again, giving in to my exhaustion.

The ice finally gives way to snow during the night, leaving us stranded without a cell phone or any form of communication… or distractions. It's just us, making the best of a bad situation. Luckily, she uses gas for her stove and water heater, so we don't have to worry about how we're going to shower or cook.

We spend the next two days forming our own little routine around the house. Each morning, she curls up at the end of the sofa and reads a book, while I work on crossword puzzles from the old newspapers. I love watching her read. She shows a thousand emotions with just her facial expressions. She bites her lip when she reads a part she likes. It is so damn cute. I ask her to tell me about it, and her face turns pink, letting me know exactly what she's reading.

When things get too quiet, I coax her into telling me funny things that happened to her when she was a kid, which leads me to share some stories of my own. I'm not even sure how it happens. I tell her things I haven't ever told anyone before. When she shares something funny, I find ways to pester her, pushing her buttons until she smiles. I could spend an eternity listening to her laugh. Usually, being cooped up like this would drive me crazy, but I can't remember when I've enjoyed spending so much time with another person.

Her dad has come by twice to check on her. The man is obviously proud of his daughter. He lights up as soon as she walks into the room. He brought Ana some supplies from the farm and helped her gather up more firewood. He sits and talks with us for a while, and even shares a few stories about Ana that she wasn't exactly expecting him to tell. I've come to enjoy his little visits.

I wish I could say the same for her buddy, Steven. He came by earlier today, and he made it clear that he still wasn't happy about me being here. I can't say that I blame the guy. I know he loves her. Hell. Who wouldn't love her? She's pretty fucking amazing.

Every minute I spend with her makes me want her even more. Her body calls out to me, taunting me, without her even knowing it. I need to own her body, to dominate her. I want to taste the salt of her skin, to tangle my fingers in her hair as I press the smooth curves of her body against me.

"What is your most embarrassing moment?" she asks, pulling me from my thoughts. It is getting late, but neither of us is really tired.

"What?" I ask. I look over to her, wondering where that question came from. She's just put another log on the fire, and she's smiling as she gets into the bed.

"Your most embarrassing moment… what is it?" she repeats as she pulls the covers over her.

"Where did that come from?" I ask, walking over to her.

"Just curious," she says as I lay down beside her.

"I'd have to say when you tried to get me to take a piss in that fucking bedpan," I tell her with a smile. There is no way I'll ever tell her what it really is.

"Oh, come on. I'm sure you can do better than that!" she says, giggling. She gets quiet and then says, "Mine is awful. I don't think I'll ever forget it."

"Alright, let's hear it." I roll to my side, so I am facing her. I love how she brings her stories to life with her facial expressions while she talks.

"It was during my gross anatomy class. We were bombarded with pictures of cadavers and videos of operations that showed proper dissection techniques.

They were trying to prepare us for the first time we used a scalpel on a real person. I'd been studying those textbooks and videos for weeks, and I had convinced myself that I was ready. I really, really thought I was prepared for anything. We were escorted into the lab and assigned our cadavers. My partner and I were a little nervous, but mostly we were excited. It was the first real step to becoming a doctor. We walked over to our assigned table, and I pulled back the nylon sheet that covered the body.... I wasn't as prepared as I thought. Our cadaver was uncircumcised. I'd never seen one on a real person before, and my eyes were drawn to it. I couldn't hide my curiosity. My partner noticed me leaning in for a closer look, and immediately started making fun of me about it. For the next two semesters, everyone called me *Skin*."

"Skin?" I'm not expecting that and can't help but laugh loudly. Then, I say it again just to make her smile. She is obviously extremely smart, but there is such an innocence to her. The expressions she makes with her eyes and mouth mesmerize me. She is beautiful and doesn't even know it.

"Stop! It was awful. I couldn't live it down," she scoffs with a serious look on her face.

"Yeah, that one is pretty bad. You win," I tell her, laughing under my breath. She continues to surprise me. I have never felt the way she makes me feel. She fascinates me in ways I cannot even begin to comprehend. I want her so much I can barely stand it.

"Stop laughing! It's not funny," she says, smiling

wide. When I don't stop, she hits my arm playfully and throws the covers off of her legs. The room falls silent when she starts to get out of the bed. She looks back to me, her eyes roaming over my bare chest. There is no mistaking the desire that fills her eyes, and right then, I know she wants me just as much as I want her.

"Come here," I demand. Her head cocks to the side like she isn't sure what I just said. "Come… here."

Her eyes lock on mine as she slowly leans over to me, giving me the only reassurance I need. Wanting to close the distance between us, my hands reach for the nape of her neck, pulling her over to me. I want to take my time with her, enjoy every second of her touch, but I can't stop myself. I'm lost the minute her lips touch mine. The sweet taste and warm, wet heat of her mouth drives me wild. As soon as she parts her lips for me, I can't hold back. My fingers dig into her flesh as the kiss becomes urgent and fills with uncontrollable need. A deep moan vibrates through her chest, encouraging me to give her more. Her fingers dive into my hair, her nails lightly dragging across the back of my neck. Her touch fuels my desire, taking me to the brink of insanity.

I reach for the hem of her t-shirt and gently slip it over her head. A low hiss slips through my clenched teeth as I notice that she isn't wearing a bra. I relish the sight of her flawless round breasts. I hadn't been able to get them out of my mind since I'd gotten a glimpse of them that day in the shower. Even in my dreams, I never imagined they'd be so perfect. I lean over her, resting my hips between her legs as her head falls back. Her hair fans out over her pillow, and she looks up at me, her green eyes glowing with lust. My fingers trail down the curve of her hips, softly slipping them inside her pajama pants. I rake my fingertips across her soft skin as I slowly lower them down her long, slender legs. Her hands dig into my biceps as I press my hard cock against her. I want to feel her… to see if she is already wet for me. I growl with approval as she raises her hips, increasing the friction between us. Her hands drop to my waist, and I feel her tug at the drawstrings of my sweats. I lift up as she eagerly pulls them down, leaving her lace panties as the only thing that separates us.

I let my eyes roam over her body, taking in every line and curve. Fuck. Every inch of her is perfect, and I am awestruck, unable to believe that she is about to be mine.

"Dillon?" she calls out to me as she lightly presses her hands against my chest.

"I want you, Ana. I've wanted you since the moment I first saw you. I can't wait to make you mine," I tell her as I lower my mouth to her ear. Goosebumps rise up along her skin when I whisper, "All of you… will… be… *mine*." She gasps with surprise as I reach for her lace panties and rip them from her body. With no more barriers, I rub my throbbing cock across her wet clit, taunting her with my metal piercing. I grasp her breast in my hand, circling her nipple with my tongue, feeling it become hard by my touch. She lowers her hand between us and runs her fingers up and down my hard shaft. The tip of her finger slowly brushes over my piercing, reminding me of the expression on her face when she first saw it. There's no doubt that she's curious about it, and I'm looking forward to showing her just how good it can feel.

CHAPTER 10

ANA

MY BODY IS in sensory overload, and I can't imagine feeling anything better. His touch scorches my skin, leaving me burning for more. My eyes roam over the beautiful ink that covers the muscles of his chest. The anticipation of having him inside me is driving me insane. The bristles of his beard scratch against my skin as he softly kisses his way down my stomach. He rests his head between my legs and places his hands under my ass, pulling me closer to him. His mouth feels warm and wet against my skin, taking my breath away with each stroke of his tongue. He torments my clit, sending electric shocks through my body. My nails rake through his hair as my moans fill the room. My body responds to his touch, taking me to a level of ecstasy I never knew was even possible. My release inches closer as he thrusts his fingers inside me, urging me to give him what my body wants. Pleasure flows through me, overcoming me, causing my whole body to shake uncontrollably as he sucks and nips at my clit with his tongue, intensifying my orgasm.

Before I can pull myself back to reality, he shifts his body between my legs. He looks down at me, his eyes full of desire as he rubs his hard cock along my entrance, driving me wild with need. I can't take it anymore. I want him… now.

"Please," I beg, not caring about the consequences.

A deep growl vibrates through his chest as he listens to my plea and enters me, driving deep inside. My nails dig into his back, and I cry out as he pushes through my hymen. I was totally unprepared for the searing pain of it tearing, and Dillon is caught off guard by my body's response. He doesn't move as my body adjusts to the fullness of him inside me. His eyes roam over my face, searching for answers that I am not ready to give.

"Ana?" he questions.

I know he's just realized that this is my first time, and I'm almost scared to look at him. I feel awkward and ashamed that I didn't tell him, but I don't want him to stop. I wrap my legs around his waist, holding him in place.

"Fuck, Ana. Why didn't you tell me?" he whispers as he brushes my hair behind my ear.

"Don't stop… please, don't stop," I plead.

"You should have told me, angel," he says softly. "I don't want to hurt you."

"You aren't," I tell him, trying to reassure him. I need him to know that I trust him and know he would never intentionally hurt me. "I want this with you more than anything," I beg. "You're an unexpected gift in my life, and there's no one in this world I'd rather share this moment with. I am falling for you… more every minute that we're together."

He finally begins to move… slow and tender, giving me time to adjust to the feeling of him inside me. His eyes are locked on mine, searching for any sign that I am in pain. The discomfort subsides, and I begin to relax. My body slowly starts to respond to him as tingles of excitement creep over me. I find myself craving more. I want him to give me all he has without worrying. I lift my hips, trying to encourage him to go deeper… harder, but he continues his slow, gentle rhythm.

I'm becoming frustrated, so I try once more to encourage him by tightening my legs around his waist and rocking against him. I hope that he will finally give me what I so desperately need.

When he pulls back, I cry out, "Dillon, please!"

"You're so fucking tight, Ana," he moans as he grinds his hips against mine. "Fuck!" he growls as he finally gives in and thrusts deep inside me. Each move he makes is more intense than the last. My eyes clench shut and my head falls back as he continues to increase his rhythm. The friction of his piercing against my g-spot causes chills to run down the back of my spine. His teeth rake over my breast as he takes my nipple in his mouth. Every nerve in my body is reacting to his touch, and I am unable to hold back. My breath quickens, and the muscles in my stomach constrict as the intensity of my orgasm builds within me. A deep groan vibrates through his throat as his body continues to pound into mine. I fight to catch my breath as my mind goes blank and my body takes over. My orgasm causes me to tighten around him, and my pussy explodes. My arms wrap around his neck, and I feel his breath against my chest as he drives deeper inside me, finally getting his own release.

Every muscle in my body relaxes as he begins to softly kiss my neck and shoulder. He lifts up and looks over to me, checking to see if I'm okay. I smile, trying to ease his concern. "That was amazing," I tell him, resting the palm of my hand on his cheek. "Thank you."

He looks at me bewildered and says, "Stay put. I'll be right back." He eases himself off of the bed and pulls on his drawstring pants. My eyes are completely focused on him as I watch him grab a candle and walk down the hall. I hear him stumbling around in the bathroom just before I hear the water running in the tub. He's gone several minutes before he walks back into the living room.

He reaches out his hand and asks, "You ready?"

"Ready?"

"Come on," he says as he takes my hand, lifting me up from the bed. He gently pulls me down the hall and into the bathroom. The room is filled with candles, and the tub is filling up with warm water.

"It will help," he whispers as he motions for me to get into the tub. I nod and slowly lower myself into the hot water. Once I'm in to my shoulders, I close my eyes and let the water ease my aching body. I look up when I hear his hand drop into the water. He takes the wash-cloth and gently begins to run it across my body, caressing me ever so softly.

"I got carried away and didn't use a condom. I want you to know that I don't normally do that. We need to figure out some kind of birth control…" he starts.

"I'm on the shot. It helps with my cycle, so we're covered," I tell him, but I continue to avoid looking at him. I keep my head down as the reality of my actions and the feelings I shared really begin to sink in.

"Stop," he says, taking hold of my face and forcing me to look him in the eye. "Ana, look at me. I don't do relationships. Never have. But the second I caught sight of you and those gorgeous green eyes, I knew you were my angel. I meant it when I told you you're mine…. Every part of you is mine. I take care of what's mine, Ana, and it's my turn to take care of *you*," he says, never taking his eyes from mine as he moves in to kiss me with a passion that consumes me.

CHAPTER 11

SHEPPARD

OVER THE PAST few months, I've watched my brothers lose themselves in the women they love. Their worlds have been turned upside down, and they love it. I never thought that would be something that I'd want or truly need, but after spending the last couple of weeks here with Ana, I can't imagine my life without her. She's more than I could have asked for, and she's mine. I meant what I told her… I take care of what's mine. I'm going to make things right for her again. She deserves to have the life she's always dreamed of, she deserves to get what she's worked so hard for, and I'm going to make sure she has it.

By the time we wake up the next morning, the power has come back on. We spend the morning putting everything back in its right place and making breakfast. While she gets dressed, I make us some scrambled eggs and toast. We are running low on groceries, but I hate the thought of either one of us leaving. I like spending time with her, and I'm not ready for it to end.

"What's cooking, good looking?" Ana asks as she

walks into the kitchen. She takes my breath away. Even in her blue sweatshirt and jeans, she looks amazing. Her hair is pulled up on top of her head in some kind of twist, and she barely has any makeup on. Irresistible.

"Nothing much. Eggs and toast is about all we have left," I tell her. The clothes her dad brought me aren't exactly my style, but Ana doesn't seem to mind as she gives me an appreciative glance or two. I admit that I like it when she looks at my ass. She tries to be discreet, but I always know when she's checking me out.

"Hopefully I'll be able to get out later and do a little shopping," she replies.

"No rush. We can make do." I grab a plate, fill it with eggs, and hand it over to her. We are just sitting down to eat when there's a knock at the front door. I look over towards the door and see Ana's dad standing there. He stomps the snow off of his boots before he comes in and says, "It's a mess out there."

Before I have a chance to offer him some breakfast, the sound of another set of boots stomping on the front porch draws my attention. I look up to find Steven walking into the kitchen. Damn.

"Steven needs to borrow your car for a little while," her dad announces. "I'd take him, but I have to feed the horses and clear off some of the trees that fell during the storm."

"What's wrong with your car?" Ana asks.

"The battery is shot on mine. I just need to run into town and get another one," Steven explains.

"Okay. Can you grab me a few things while you're in

town?" she asks.

"Sure. Just make me a list," Steven replies as he helps himself to a plate of eggs. He looks over to me and says, "These are great. Did you add cheese or something?"

"Yeah, and some garlic."

"Awesome," he mumbles as he eats another big mouthful.

Ana's dad turns to Steven and says, "If you have time, swing by and pick her up a new phone while you're in town. I called and told them she 'lost' her old one, so it shouldn't be a problem."

"What happened? Did you drop it in the toilet again?" he asks, laughing.

"No, smartass… I dropped it," Ana says as she looks over to me and winks.

After she writes a few things down, she hands her list to Steven. "You sure this is all you need?" he asks.

"That should do it," Ana tells him as she takes her last bite of eggs. "Let me grab my keys. Be careful out there. The roads will be bad for a few days."

"Ana, this isn't my first rodeo. I know how to drive on the snow." He stands up and places his now empty plate in the sink. She tosses him her keys, and he says, "Thanks. I'll be careful." Then, he turns and walks out the door.

Ana's dad stays and talks for a few more minutes and then tells us he has to get back to the farm. I offer to go with him, but he refuses. I have a feeling he knows I'm not completely healed, and I wouldn't be much help. I'm sure he doesn't want me to get in his way.

"Wanna watch a movie to take your mind off of things?" Ana asks.

"Why don't we go for a walk? Get out of the house for a while."

"Give me a minute to grab us some coats. I think I have one of Dad's old hunting jackets that will fit you in the back closet," she says as she heads down the hall, looking excited about our walk. She quickly returns with her arms full of clothes. She drops everything on the sofa, looks at me, and says, "Wrap up. It's really cold out."

I shake my head and grab a green down jacket and a pair of black gloves. Then, I watch as she transforms herself. She puts on so many layers she looks like a walking laundry basket. Damn, she's so cute.

"Ana, it's not that cold," I laugh.

"You say that now. No complaining when you're freezing out there," she mumbles as she puts on her toboggan.

"I'll survive," I insist as I grab her hand and pull her into me, placing my lips against hers. She moans lightly as I wrap my arms around her shoulders, the kiss becoming more intense. I feel myself getting carried away, so with some willpower, I pull back and release her from our intimate embrace. All I can think about is how I want to drag her down the hall and make love to her again… and I want to fuck her, hard and unrestrained, but I fight the urge, knowing that she still needs time to recover from last night. I grab hold of her hand and lead her towards the door, "Let's go if we have to." I say the words as if this is a chore, but truth be known, I'm excited.

I was right. It is so good to be out of the house. We spend several hours walking down by the tranquil lake. All the wildlife is scurrying around and digging for food. They look happy, playing in the pure white, soft snow. We watch as they run and hide, being spooked by their own shadows, leaving thousands of little footprints in the untouched carpet of snow. Everything is covered in white… a true winter wonderland created by Nature herself.

Gripping my hand tighter, Ana leads me to the spot where she found me. I don't recognize any of it. Her face is filled with sadness as she starts to tell me all about it. I listen for a few minutes, and when I can't stand to hear any more, I decide it's time for a distraction. I bend down and scoop up a handful of snow. She doesn't even notice as she continues telling me the story of her rescue, not just talking but reliving it with all of her cute mannerisms and arm gestures. I remove my gloves and use my bare hands to form the snow into a perfect ball. She's still staring at the water when I throw the snowball at her chest. Snow covers the front of her jacket, and the look of shock on her face is perfect and makes me laugh. She stands frozen, staring at me, unable to believe that I just creamed her with a snowball. That makes me laugh even more. I am bent over laughing when I feel the cold sting of ice glide down my back.

I instantly stand up straight and give her a look that lets her know she's about to get it. She takes off running, and I can hear her nervous laugh echo through the trees. I reach down to grab more snow to make another snowball and start tracking her down. "You're going to pay for that, Angel."

"I'm sorry!!!" she shouts as she runs back up the hill. I'm having a hard time catching her, but I finally reach her. I throw my arm around her waist and collapse to the ground, bringing her with me. The snow crunches and compacts under us, cushioning our fall as I pull her on top of me.

Our laughter is silenced when we hear Ana's name being called from back at the house. I look up the hill and see Ana's dad frantically running in our direction. The horrified look on his face tells me that something isn't right.

"Daddy? What's wrong?"

Everything falls silent as her father tries to catch his breath and says, "There's been an accident." He walks over to Ana and places his hand on her shoulder. "It's Steven."

"What kind of accident? Is he okay?" she asks, her voice cracking as tears fill her eyes.

Her father looks to the ground, and I know it's going to be bad. "It doesn't look good, honey. They had to take him to the hospital."

"What?? They can't take him there! Something…" Ana begins.

"Ana, they didn't have a choice. He was in bad shape, and the paramedics had to get him to the closest hospital," her father says as he steps closer to her.

"But what if they do something to him?! We can't trust them!"

"Ana, they may be crazy, but they aren't stupid. I don't think they're going to do anything. They already think you know something," he says as he places his hand on her elbow. "It will be okay."

"I don't like it," she says with concern.

"I know, but I'll keep an eye on things," he promises, trying to reassure her.

I take her hand in mine as we follow him up the hill. We go straight to his truck, so he can take us to see Steven. He explains everything on the way, telling us it was one of the worst car accidents he'd ever seen. Apparently, Steven wasn't able to stop the car and was hit by a semi-truck. One of Ana's father's friends from the police department called him as soon as it'd happened. When her dad arrived on the scene, the paramedics told him that they didn't expect Steven to live. In fact, they were amazed he was alive when they cut him out of the wreck. He had lost a lot of blood and had a fractured left femur. I could see the dismay on Ana's face; one of the drawbacks to being a surgeon is that they know when the situation is bad.

I know she's worried about Steven being at the same hospital that has caused her so much trouble, but it couldn't be helped. Steven needed immediate medical attention, and there wasn't any other option. Still, she doesn't like it. She knows there's something going on, and she doesn't trust anyone working there. Hopefully, it won't be an issue, but either way, I trust Ana's dad. I know he will keep an eye on things.

As we make our way into the main part of town, something just doesn't seem right to me. Unlike the back roads, all of these roads are clear. It looks like they've been clear for a while, so it doesn't make any sense for Steven to have had problems stopping the car. After listening to the rest of the story from Ana's dad, and judging by the fact that Steven doesn't come across as clumsy, I figured there had to be another explanation.

"Where is Ana's car now?" I ask.

"The wrecker service came and got it."

"Can you drop me off there? I'll meet you both at the hospital after I look it over."

Her father nods. Ana looks over to me, and I'm sure she wonders why I want to see her car. There's no reason for me to worry her, so I keep my thoughts to myself. When he pulls into the lot, I squeeze her hand, give her a reassuring smile, and get out of the truck. They leave me there so they can go check on Steven.

Her car is sitting out front, waiting to be taken to the scrapyard. It was totaled, unable to sustain the massive impact, and there is no way it can be salvaged. I waste no time and begin looking the car over. It's a complete fucking wreck, but I know what I'm looking for. After just a few minutes, I'm able to locate the problem. The soft copper brake pipe had been tampered with. It was a professional job, not just a cut. The pipe had been warmed and pinned, then sealed. When pressure was applied, the pipe blew. Anger surges through me as my doubts are confirmed. This was no fucking accident.

I'm done with this shit. It's time to find out what the hell is really going on. First, I need to look into this Jason guy. From everything Ana's told me, I know he's behind this. It's time to get Ana to the clubhouse. She's it for me, and there's no way I'm going to take a chance on something happening to her. I know in my gut that she isn't safe here.

I get a cab to take me over to the hospital. Ana is talking with one of the doctors, so I take that opportunity to talk to her dad.

"Her brakes were tampered with, and it was someone who knew what they were doing," I tell him.

"Are you sure?" he asks with panic.

"No doubt. The car is totaled, but there is no way that the crash was an accident. Someone was trying to kill to Ana."

"Damn it. They've gone too far now."

"You're right. I know you don't really know me, but I do have your daughter's best interests at heart." He nods in agreement as I continue talking. "That's why I'm going to take her back to my clubhouse with me. I need to know that she's safe while I figure out what to do about this."

His demeanor immediately changes as he shouts, "No! No, she can stay with me. I can look after her. I don't need you getting in the middle of all this. She's my daughter, Dillon."

"Too late, sir. I'm in it now… whether you want me to be or not, and I'm going to take care of it. You can count on that, but there's no way I'm leaving her here.

It's just too dangerous," I explain.

I can tell he isn't happy when he speaks again. "I'm just supposed to be okay with you taking my Ana to some clubhouse in Tennessee? You've only known her a few days, and we don't know anything about you!"

The hospital is getting busy, and it's hard to talk privately. I do understand where he's coming from. She is his daughter, the person he cares the very most about, and he feels like I'm trying to take her away from him.

He clears his throat and continues, "I like you, Dillon. You seem like a good man, but I'm not just letting you take her off to god knows where. I need a lot more information and reassurance if you expect me to be okay with this."

"I understand, sir, and you're right. All I ask is that you give me a chance to make this right for her. She deserves to have the life she's always dreamed of. I'm not going to let them take that away from her."

Ana's dad sighed, then started to talk more slowly and with less agitation, "You may be right, Dillon. This trouble Ana is in, whatever it is, has some connection to that hospital. I know that the people after her have a lot of power and influence, not to mention, money. A safe place out of town is probably what she needs. I'm just worried about her."

"I can tell you this… I know that Ana is special to you, and I know you only want the best for her. I feel the same way. Without even meaning to, that woman stole my heart. She holds it in the palm of her hand. I'll do anything in the world for her. I give you my word… Ana will be safe with me."

CHAPTER 12

ANA

MY HEAD IS spinning. Everything is happening so damn fast, and I haven't had time to really think. I'm in dad's truck with Dillon, heading to his clubhouse in Tennessee. I didn't want to go. I tried to explain to Dad that I couldn't just leave Steven. I didn't trust the people at that hospital, but he wouldn't listen. He said Dillon was right. They both decided that this is the best way to ensure my safety. As much as I hate leaving right now, I know Dad will watch over Steven. He'll make sure that nothing happens to him. Steven is like a son to him, and he'll make sure he has everything he needs. He promised to keep me updated on everything, even calling a few minutes ago to tell me that they moved him out of the ICU. I am so relieved that he is doing better. I just hope he will forgive me for leaving him.

When Dillon notices the worried look on my face, he takes my hand in his and says, "Trust me, Angel… I told you that you were mine. The minute I claimed you, you became part of our MC family. That means more than you realize. We take care of our own, Ana. My brothers and I will do whatever it takes to keep you safe." There is something in his voice that convinces me. I truly believe that he is the answer to my prayers, and I have to trust that he will take care of me.

"Okay," I tell him. "Thank you for all this."

"Nothing to thank me for, Ana. You're it for me, baby." The truck falls silent after that. Both of us are lost in our own thoughts as we drive along the Interstate. My nerves go into overdrive as we cross over the bridge into Paris. Butterflies start fluttering all through my stomach. I try to calm myself by looking out the window, distracting my mind from all the anxiety I feel. My eyes are drawn to the beautiful lake, running for miles on both sides of the bridge. It's gorgeous. Just as I think we are about to drive into town, Dillon turns off on a side road that looks a lot like the road I live on. After several sharp curves and turns, he pulls into a long driveway. There is a large gate, but it's open, allowing us to enter the almost empty parking lot.

This place is nothing like I'd imagined it would be. I've never seen anything quite like it before. There is a huge car garage attached to an amazing rustic warehouse with a silver tin roof. The large windows make it look more like a home rather than a clubhouse. Dillon puts the truck in park and takes a deep breath before he looks over to me and asks, "You ready for this?"

"Ready as I'll ever be."

"Ana," he says as he takes my chin and turns me to look him in the eye. "Do you trust me?"

"You know I do."

"This club is my world. The day I told you that you were mine, you became my world as well. Ana, you're going to see and hear things that you may not understand. There are going to be questions I can't answer.... I need you to trust me."

"What does that mean?"

"I know I told you about the club, but we don't do things the way you're used to. When I made you mine, I claimed you. To my club, that makes you my Old Lady."

"Explain?"

"In my world, that means I've made you mine... that makes you my wife."

As soon as the words come from his mouth, I feel suspended in time. The whole world seems to stop, and everything around us stills. I love the thought of being his, and the fact that he is claiming me like this makes me feel complete in a way I've never known.

I wrap my arms around his neck, pulling him to me, and say, "Thank you." My lips crash against his, showing him how much his words mean to me. His arms wrap around my waist, lifting me off the ground. When he releases me, he looks at me and smiles. I can't believe he's mine.

He slowly lowers me to the ground and says, "Come on. Let's do this, Angel." He takes my hand, leading me towards the clubhouse.

I follow him around to the side entrance, and as soon as he opens the door, my hearts starts pounding in my chest. I can hear the faint rumble of voices as we step into the clubhouse, but I can't make out what they're saying. The muted smell of beer and leather fill the air, and my eyes quickly wander around the room. It looks like a regular bar… several people are sitting with their backs to us at the L-shaped counter drinking beer and talking to one another. There's a beautiful redhead standing behind the bar, serving everyone drinks. She is the first one to notice us. She freezes, staring at Dillon like she's seeing a ghost. Her eyes are filled with disbelief as she stands motionless and stares at him. She's absolutely dumbfounded.

"Sheppard?" she whispers. In a trance, she says his name again… louder. "Sheppard?"

All at once, the men who were occupied with their own conversations stop talking and turn to look at us. Their faces are marked with shock and confusion as they sit frozen in their seats. Dillon takes a deep breath and starts walking towards them, pulling me along with him.

"What the fuck?" several of the men mumble as we approach. They are more than stunned. The man they thought had been dead for weeks is walking into the room like nothing has happened, and they just can't make sense of it.

"Fucking hell… Shep, is that really you?" one of the men asks as we stop in front of him. He's tall, with a muscular build, and he's wearing a black leather jacket.

"None other," Dillon replies.

Sheppard? I haven't heard that name before.

I glance over to Dillon, and he's smiling. "You miss me, Renegade?" he asks with pure happiness in his voice.

The man he just called Renegade quickly stands up

and hugs him tightly. "I can't believe it, man. We thought you were dead."

"I would be if it wasn't for Ana," he says, motioning his hand over in my direction. Renegade releases Dillon from his bear hug and looks over to me.

"You found him?" he asks.

"I did. He wasn't exactly in good shape, but he was just stubborn enough to live through it," I tell him.

"That's him alright. Stubborn as hell, but damn… it's good to have him back."

Excitement crackles through the air as the other men all take their turns giving Dillon hugs and slapping him on the back. I try to make note of each of their names as they talk… Doc, Otis, Bulldog, but it's no use. They're all in shock, talking a mile a minute. It's just too hard to keep up with what they are all saying. Someone else walks into the room, and everyone falls silent. He's tall, too, but that's not what makes him intimidating. His posture commands respect, but the emotion that spreads across his face leads me to believe that he has a softer side. All eyes are on him as he approaches Dillon.

"Bishop…" Dillon says as he steps over to him. "It's good to see you, brother."

Bishop doesn't say a word as he wraps his arms around him, hugging him tightly. They stand frozen in their embrace for several moments, neither of them speaking as they hold on to one another.

His voice filled with anguish, Bishop says, "I've prayed that you'd make your way back to us. Never stopped praying, brother."

I can't stop the tears from streaming down my face as I watch them like this. It reminds me of a father finding out his son is still alive, and my heart just can't take it. There is so much love in this room, and I can see why Dillon cares so much about each of them.

Bishop finally pulls back from Dillon and gives him a stern look. "Why didn't you contact us? You owed us that much. We've spent the last few weeks thinking you were dead."

"I couldn't. I gave my word, Bishop. I'll explain everything later," Dillon says as he reaches out for me, tucking me into his side, and says, "This is my Ana. She's the reason I'm standing here right now."

I brush the tears from my eyes as Bishop looks at me. He cocks his head to the side as he looks me up and down. It's like he's trying to make sense of why I'm here, and he doesn't know what to say.

"She saved my life, Bishop," Dillon tells him as he leans in and kisses me on my forehead.

"Ana… don't know how you did it. Just fucking glad you did. Things haven't been the same here without him around," Bishop tells me as he runs his hand down my arm. His eyes are filled with gratitude.

"I can imagine. I've seen it for myself… he can be a handful," I tell him as I lightly squeeze Dillon's waist.

"You have no fucking idea," Bishop says with a smile.

Dillon clears his throat and turns to Bishop to say, "I need to talk to you about a few things when you get a minute."

"Why don't you go get Ana settled in your room and meet me back in the office?"

"I'll be there in ten," Dillon says. He motions his head towards a long hallway, and I follow him as he leads me down to his room. The hallway is filled with doors, and I assume that they are all bedrooms. We reach the fourth door on the right, and Dillon opens it, pulling me inside. Once we are inside, he shuts the door with his foot and looks at me intently. He tugs me over to him, pressing his lips against mine. My mouth instantly curves into a smile as I think back to everything that just happened. Those men are crazy about him, just like me. I can see why he's so happy to be back. Dillon looks down at me with his eyebrows furrowed.

"Sheppard?" I ask. "Why did they call you Sheppard?"

"It's just a nickname. I guess we all have one," he tells me.

"Why Sheppard?" I ask.

"I don't know. It's something Bishop came up with when I first came here. It had something to do with my military training at Sheppard's Air Force Academy. I told him some things that happened while I was there, and the next thing I knew, he was calling me Sheppard. He says it suits me," Dillon explains.

"Should I call you Sheppard?" I ask.

"No."

"I mean… I don't mind. I want to do the right thing with all this and…."

"No."

He leans down and kisses me softly, stopping me from saying anything else. I slip my arms around his waist, enjoying our brief moment alone together, knowing he has to leave. He pulls me closer, deepening the kiss. A part of me wishes he could just stay here with me. I feel so safe wrapped in his arms. Everything around us seems to disappear when he is close to me. He looks down at me and says, "I've got to go talk to Bishop. Try to make yourself comfortable. I'll show you around and introduce you to everybody when I get back."

"Okay."

"Ana?" He looks at me with such sincerity I think I may melt. "Thank you."

He kisses me one last time before he turns to leave. I watch as he closes the door behind him, and I know right then… there's nothing I wouldn't do for that man. Nothing.

CHAPTER 13
SHEPPARD

"TELL ME WHY you didn't call us, Shep. I need you to make me understand," Bishop says as he stands in front of me with his arms crossed.

"It was Ana's father. He'd seen the news, and he had conditions for his daughter's safety. I couldn't guarantee that things were clear with the club, and he was concerned. He didn't want me bringing any more trouble to Ana. He said that they'd take care of me and help me heal if I gave my word that I wouldn't contact anyone," I explained.

"Your brothers come first, Shep. You should've called."

"I had to go with my gut on this one, man. I gave her father my word, Bishop. His daughter had just saved my life, and I couldn't risk her safety."

"You're really serious about this girl?" Bishop asks me.

"Yeah, Bishop. I've never wanted anything more. I'm claiming her. She's mine, and I'll do everything it takes to keep her safe. The thought of someone trying to hurt her is eating me up inside."

"We'll figure all this out, but we need to talk to Ana. Get the facts straight. She may know more than she realizes. We need names… Jason, his parents, and these patients. Anyone that might lead us to some answers."

"She has notes or something where she kept track of everything. I'm sure she brought it with her."

"Good. We'll need to see it," he tells me.

"Where do we start?"

"We'll need to get Crack Nut in on this. He's our best bet at finding out what's really going on at that hospital," Bishop says as he steps closer to me. "He had a really hard time when we couldn't find you. He never gave up looking."

"Seriously?" I ask. "I guess that doesn't surprise me. He's always been determined."

"It's more than that, Shep, and you know it. You'll never know how hard it was for all of us to leave you. We searched for hours, but the current was just too fucking fast, brother. You vanished. In a matter of seconds, you were just gone. None of us wanted to give up hope, but Crack Nut took it to another level. He spent hours checking every hospital in the state, searching for any John Does that may have turned up. He even monitored police scanners in case someone came across your body. He just couldn't let it go. We all thought if you were out there, he'd be the one to find you."

"I'm sure he would have found me sooner or later."

"Maybe…. We're all just glad you're back. We'll get

this shit sorted with Ana. You've got my word," Bishop says as he reaches out to shake my hand. "What about your cut? Never seen you here without it."

"Gone. Lost it in the lake," I explain.

"I'll call Louise. She'll take care of it."

"Thanks, Bishop… for everything."

"I'm calling the guys in for church tonight at seven. Let everyone know what's going on," he announces. "Need you there."

I nod. I've missed meeting with the guys. It will be good to see everyone, and it will give me a chance to introduce Ana. They all need to know she's mine, and she's now part of the club.

"I'll be there," I tell him before I turn to leave. "It's good to be back, Pres." I shut his door and head back to my room to find Ana. I need her. Now.

She's lying on my bed half asleep when I walk into my room and shut the door. She looks so peaceful lying there, like an angel sent here just for me. Without saying a word, I kneel down at the foot of the bed and pull her over to the edge. Her eyes drift open, and she quietly watches me as I begin unbuttoning her jeans and slowly slide them down her legs. I need to taste her, sweet and warm. Her eyes lock on mine as my rough hands trace along her legs, gliding tenderly over her calves to her knees until I reach between her thighs. My thumb brushes back and forth across her clit, tormenting her through the thin layer of her pink lace panties. She lifts her hips, pushing against my hand to increase the pressure of my touch.

"Easy, Angel. I'll give you what you need," I assure her. My fingers slip into her panties, pulling them down her body. They fall useless to the floor along with her jeans as I lower my mouth down between her legs. She gasps as my tongue skims across her clit, pressing against her nub. I tease back and forth in a gentle rhythm against her sensitive flesh. Her fingers delve into my hair, gripping me tightly. Her hips squirm below me as I increase the pressure against her clit. When her breath becomes ragged, I thrust my middle finger deep inside her, twirling against her g-spot with a slow and steady pace. I add a second finger, driving deeper, sliding farther inside her as she tenses around me. Her body rocks against my hand, increasing the friction as she tries to take control.

"Not yet," I demand, and knowing it will drive her wild, I slow my pace. I torment her with my resistance, so she will remember that I am the one with the power to satisfy her needs. She groans loudly, filling the room with the sounds of her frustration. I smile knowing that she's learning… she'll see that I will give her everything she needs.

Goosebumps prickle across her skin as I nip and suck the inside of her thigh, just inches away from her clit. Her hips lift up from the bed, begging for me to give her more. I finally give in and drive my fingers deep inside her pussy, twirling and caressing her delicate flesh. Her body shudders beneath me as I continue to fuck her with my fingers. She releases my hair, and her hands drop to the bed, digging into the sheets as she begins to quiver uncontrollably. I know she's getting close, and I can't help the satisfied grin that crosses my face knowing that she's about to cum.

"That's it, Angel. Cum for me," I demand.

Her head thrashes from side to side as I continue to curl my fingers inside her, teasing that spot that's driving her wild. She murmurs my name over and over as the muscles in her pussy clench around me. I continue to lick and suck at her clit until her body begins to come down from its high.

Before she has time to fully recover, I drop my jeans to the floor, and without even trying to move her, I settle between her legs. My knees barely hit the edge of the bed, but I don't give a fuck. I just need her, all of her… every fucking inch of her. I want to feel her, let the world around me disappear while I claim her body, making her mine in the most primal way. Her arms wrap around my neck as my piercing drags across her clit. She looks up at me longingly, her green eyes glowing with lust. She lays there just begging to be taken, and my heart stops beating in my chest. Fuck! My pulse begins racing with need as my cock presses against her entrance. She shifts her hips, forcing the head of my cock inside her. I slowly ease myself deep inside, inch by inch, giving her time to adjust to me. Her hips buck beneath me.

"Yes!" she cries as I fill her completely.

"You're mine, Angel. All mine," I whisper in her ear as I slide the soft white t-shirt up over her stomach just enough to reveal her perfect round breasts. I take her nipple in my mouth. I can hear the pounding of her heart as my tongue twirls around her breast, her breath quickening as my teeth rake across her flesh.

"Yes," she groans, her legs instinctively wrapping around my waist as she pulls me deeper inside her. I slowly withdraw, then gradually ease back inside her. My pace is steady and unforgiving as I tease her g-spot with the round metal ball of my piercing. My eyes wander over her beautiful body, taking in every beautiful curve of her frame. I watch her chest rise and fall with each breath she takes, each gasp of air sounding more desperate than the last. Her hips flex upwards, her tight pussy gripping firmly around my cock. I growl with satisfaction when I feel her nails rake across my spine, knowing she's just left her marks all down my back. My pace never falters as I continue to thrust inside her, over and over, constantly increasing the rhythm of my movements.

"Fuck!" I shout out as my throbbing cock demands its release too fucking soon. I want to relish the moment, but I can't hold back. She's just too fucking tight, feels too fucking good to stop. I plunge inside her again and again, feeling her pussy spasm with her impending release. My hips collide into hers, each thrust coming faster, harder with every breath I take. I want to possess her as I drive into her, again and again, and she comes around my cock. Her body jolts and writhes as her orgasm takes control of her body. My hands reach under her, lifting her ass higher so I can drive deeper inside her. Pounding into her body, I feel myself getting closer as her pussy clamps down against my cock. My dick pulses, growing harder just before I cum inside of her.

The sounds of our deep breaths fill the room as I collapse beside her on the bed and pull her up to the crook of my arm. "Ana?"

"Hmm?" she murmurs as she looks over at me with those beautiful green eyes. Damn. There's no doubt in my mind… I know I'll never feel this way about another woman.

"Getting shot may be the best thing that's ever happened to me," I tell her. She smiles and curls into my arm. I am totally in awe of this woman. I want to hold her close… protect her… possess her. Not only did she save my life, she's given me the most sacred part of herself… her body and her heart, something no man has ever had. And then, she thanked me for it. It blows me away…. I'm the one who's thankful. She's mine. She's right where she belongs, and I don't plan on ever letting her go. I will spend the rest of my life showing her how grateful I am.

CHAPTER 14
ANA

I LOVE THE sound of his laugh. I love everything about him, and the words are right there… right on the tip of my tongue. But, I just can't say them. I don't know what's stopping me, but I just can't do it. It's like something is stuck in my throat, blocking my words. There's no doubt in my mind that I love this man more than anything in this world, but something is making me hold back. Maybe it's self-preservation or something stupid like that. Hell, I don't know what it is, but lying here in his arms is the only place I ever want to be.

"You up for meeting the rest of the crew tonight?" Dillon asks as he runs his fingers through my hair, his blue eyes looking at me intently.

"Absolutely. Looking forward to it," I lie. I'm actually pretty nervous about it. I just hope I don't do or say something stupid and embarrass myself.

"I have to go meet with the guys for a little while, but afterwards, I will introduce you to everyone."

"I'd like that," I say, but my nerves are setting in. I can't blow this. It's too important.

He lifts up on his elbow and looks down at me. His eyes pierce through me like he's searching for the answer to some unknown question. "Ana?"

"What?" I ask, finally looking him in the eye.

"They are going to love you. Stop worrying about it."

"Okay."

"*Ana...*"

"I said, Okay. I'll be fine," I say, laughing.

"Good. I'm looking forward to showing you off tonight," he says as he presses his soft lips against mine. I wish we could just stay here like this for the rest of the night, but I know this is important to him.

"What time do you have to go to meet with the guys?"

He looks over at the clock and says, "In about twenty minutes. I better take a shower and get going."

"Okay. I'm going to rest a minute, and then I will get ready while you're gone," I say and pull the covers over me.

He kisses me one last time before he pulls himself up out of the bed. I can't take my eyes off of him as he walks into the bathroom. Damn. He's perfect. I throw my arm up over my eyes and try to remember what clothes I brought with me. If he is planning to show me off tonight, I want to look my best. I close my eyes and try to think of the perfect outfit, but nothing comes to mind.

My eyes fly open when I hear someone's door slam down the hall. I lift myself up on my elbows and look at the clock. Craptastic! I must have fallen asleep, and

Dillon didn't wake me up. I jump out of bed, and almost fall on my face as I stumble across our bags that are spread out on the floor. He must have brought them in while I was sleeping. Brownie points for him. I unzip my bag and search for my best pair of black skinny jeans and my favorite plaid shirt. After I get everything laid out, I rush to the shower. I have no idea when he will be back, so I don't waste any time getting ready.

I'm putting on the last bit of my makeup when Dillon walks back into the room, and he's wearing *his clothes.* Holy hell. I had no idea how hot he could look in his clothes. I'm frozen in place as my eyes roam over his body, drooling like some lovesick schoolgirl. I can't help myself. His blue jeans are resting low on his hips with rips and tears all around the knees. His button up shirt fits tight around the muscles of his chest and arms, showing off his perfectly toned body. I love the way his hair looks like he didn't do anything to it, but it looks so damn sexy all tousled around his head. Those blue eyes of his sparkle as he notices me checking him out, and yes, I am definitely checking him out. I can't believe he's mine. Without saying a word, I drop my mascara on the counter and walk over to him.

I wrap my arms around his neck and say, "You look… *hot.*"

"You think so?" he asks with a laugh.

"Absolutely."

"I still have a few of the clothes your dad gave me. I can always change…."

"Burn those clothes. Seriously. Burn them."

He leans down and whispers in my ear, "You look pretty damn hot yourself." His lips brush against my neck, sending chills down my spine. "We have to go. They're waiting for us."

"Okay. Let's do this."

He reaches for my hand and leads me out of the room. As soon as we step out, blaring music and the rumble of laughter echo down the hallway. Before I have a chance to get nervous, Dillon pulls me close to him, relieving the butterflies in my stomach. Just being close to him makes me feel better. All eyes are on us as we enter the bar.

"There he is! Get your ass over here, Shep!" shouts an older man standing by the pool table.

"Give me a minute, Doc. Gotta grab a beer," Dillon says as we walk up to the bar.

"It's about time you got here. I've been dying to meet you! Is it true? Did you really save his life?" the beautiful redhead behind the bar asks.

"Yeah. I guess I did," I tell her.

"Lily, this is Ana. Ana, this is Goliath's wife. He's the big guy over at the pool table with Doc."

"It's nice to meet you, Lily."

"Have a seat, girl. We have lots to talk about," Lily tells me as she passes us both a beer.

"You okay here for a bit? I'm gonna go talk to the guys for a minute," Dillon asks.

"I'm fine. Go ahead," I tell him, smiling.

"Go, Shep. I got her," Lily tells him. He kisses me lightly before he heads over to the guys.

"Don't run off. I'll be back in a minute," he calls back to me.

I shake my head and look back to Lily. "He's glad to be back. I think he missed it here more than he realized."

"We missed him, too. It just wasn't the same around here without him. Thanks for taking such good care of him," Lily says as she slides a beer over to one of the men sitting at the end of the counter.

"Yeah, well… it wasn't always easy. That man has a stubborn streak a mile long."

"You haven't met Goliath. He's the stubborn one," Lily says, laughing.

"Don't even start, Lily. We all know Bishop is the stubborn one," a gorgeous brunette says as she sits down beside me.

"Tessa, you have Bishop wrapped around your little finger. There's no way he's more stubborn than Goliath."

"You weren't there when we were trying to decide on a honeymoon. He has his mind set on going to Mexico, and he just won't listen to me. It's going to be a pain to get those passports," Tessa tells her.

"Yeah, well, Goliath wants me to stop working. He says that it isn't good for the baby. I'm like three months pregnant, and I feel great. I don't want to quit working. I'd lose my mind if I had to stay home all the time. You know, if he wins this one, I'll never live it down… and let's not forget the wedding. He didn't even tell me we were eloping. I thought we were going away for the weekend," Lily says as she shakes her head, but she is smiling. She may say that Goliath is stubborn, but I can tell a part of her likes it. The way her face lights up when she talks says it all. She loves him… there's no doubt.

"Yeah, you may have me there." Tessa turns to me with a bright smile and says, "You must be Ana. I've heard a lot about you. You're prettier than Bishop said. I'd say that Sheppard really lucked out."

"Thank you, Tessa. I great to finally meet you. I've heard a lot about you, and I'm looking forward to meeting your children. Dillon talks about them all the time. He thinks they're pretty awesome,' I tell her.

"Yeah, they're pretty amazing. They definitely keep me on my toes," she says as she glances over to Bishop. His eyes are locked on her. It's obvious that these two are crazy about each other.

Another lady approaches the bar and sits down by Tessa. She smiles and says, "Just wait til you have this baby. Then you'll really be a nut case. I almost feel sorry for Bishop."

"That's why I have you, Court. You will be there to keep me sane," Tessa says, laughing. Her smile is contagious. Just looking at her has me grinning from ear to ear. "Courtney, this is Ana. Shep's friend."

"Friend? …. Yeah, right. We all know it's more than that. He's head over heels over you, Ana. You got ya a good one," Courtney says as she looks over at Sheppard. "Look at the poor guy. He can't take his eyes off of her."

We all turn and look at him, and sure enough, he is staring right at me. I can't hold back my smile. That man gets to me, and I like it.

"So… is it true?" Courtney asks.

"What?" I turn back to her, trying to figure out what she's talking about.

"Does he really have one of those piercings? You know, down below?" she asks with her eyebrow perched high.

"Courtney! You can't ask her that! You'll embarrass her," Lily snaps.

"It's a simple question. You know you want to know, too, Lily. Just because you are all knocked up and happy, doesn't mean you can't be curious about another man's junk. I just want to know if it's really pierced or not," Courtney explains.

"Umm… I…" I start.

"Don't answer that," Dillon says as he leans over and rests his elbows on the bar. "Courtney, behave."

Courtney smiles and rolls her eyes, acting like she is offended, but we know she isn't. Something tells me it would take a lot to get to her. I like that about her.

"You doing okay?" Dillon asks.

"Yes, now go. Get back to your game," I tell him.

"Okay, boss," he says, but before he goes, he turns towards me and kisses me. He doesn't give me one of his soft kisses like I was expecting. Instead, his tongue brushes against my bottom lip, urging me to open my mouth. When I comply, he deepens the kiss, taking his time with me. I turn my body towards him, but he pulls away, leaving me desperate for more. I moan with disapproval when he looks down at me. "You sure you want me to go?" he teases.

I shake my head yes, but I really want him to stay. Actually, I really just want to go back to his room and spend the night making love to him.

"Stop teasing her, Shep. We still have stuff to talk about," Lily tells him.

"Can't help myself," he says as he gives me a sexy wink and turns to go back to his game. My eyes are glued to him as I watch him walk away.

"Damn, she's got it bad," Courtney snickers.

"I think it's great. Sheppard's a great guy. I'm glad he's found someone that makes him happy," Tessa tells her.

"Looks like they are both pretty damn happy," Courtney says with a smirk.

"Do you think you'll stay here?" Tessa asks.

"I guess we'll have to wait and see how this all plays out. Things in my life are a little… complicated right now."

"Things are always going to be complicated, girl. You just have to do what makes you happy," Courtney says to me.

We talk for several hours, about anything and everything. I love it. It's been so long since I've had a night out. I've never really had a group of friends like this, and it means a lot to me that they are all so friendly and open. Courtney tells me all about her awful accident and Bobby's big proposal at the movie theater. Lily shares stories about John Warren and her pregnancy, while Tessa tells us all about her wedding plans. She seems so excited that it is finally all working out. Lily also tells me all about Taylor, Renegade's fiancé. They said I would meet her tomorrow, since she's on babysitting duty tonight for John Warren. I love listening to all their wonderful stories. I'm beginning to think I would actually like staying here with Dillon.

"Will you look at what she's wearing tonight? Why does she even bother putting on any clothes at all?" Courtney says as she eyeballs a woman walking into the bar. Her hair is flowing all around her shoulders, actually covering more skin than her tiny leather tube top and miniskirt.

"At least Cindy isn't here tonight," Lily tells her.

"I'm not worried about Cindy anymore. I think she has finally gotten over her thing with Bobby...." She tries to hold back her smile as she says, "It may have had something to do with that surprise I left for her in her bed last week."

"Courtney! What did you do?" Tessa asks.

"Not saying. I don't want to hear one of your lectures. Let's just say that it was effective. That's all that really matters," Courtney explains as she watches the woman walk over to the pool table. "Umm... does Brandi know about Ana?" she asks Tessa.

Tessa turns to look in Dillon's direction and says, "Probably not. Even if she did, I doubt she'd care."

"Who is Brandi?" I ask.

"She's one of the Fallen girls. They are here for the guys when they need to let off some steam. There used to be more of them, but now most of the guys have Old Ladies," Tessa explains.

"So, Dillon has been with these women?" I ask.

None of them speak, but I know the answer. It's written all over their faces. I look back over and watch as Brandi rests her hand on Dillon's chest. Something in me snaps. I don't know what comes over me. I feel like a rabid dog stalking its prey. As soon as Brandi starts to wedge herself between his legs, I see him place his hands on her hips, pushing her back away from him. His expression is fierce as he talks to her, but she isn't taking the hint as she continues to shove her giant boobs in his face. When her hand reaches up into his hair, I'm done. In an instant, my feet have hit the floor, and I'm walking over towards them.

"Ana?" Courtney asks. I just keep walking. I'm too pissed to even think. "Ana, wait!"

I should listen to her. I should stop right here and go back to my seat at the bar, but I don't. I just keep walking over to Dillon and the two-dollar whore that's hanging all over him.

When I finally get over to them, I say, "If you want to keep your hand intact, you might want to move it.... Now."

Brandi casually turns her head to face me, and her eyes slowly roam over me from head to toe before she says, "And what are you going to do about it, sweetie?" My eyes are still trained on her hand. Her fingers are splayed across his cheek, her nails just barely touching his hair.

"There are twenty-seven bones in your hand, fourteen of those are in your fingers," I inform her.

"So?" she says, stepping closer to Dillon, egging me on.

"It hurts like hell when they break. And you're about to find out exactly how that feels, if you don't...."

"Who are *you* anyway?" she says sarcastically.

"She's..." Dillon starts.

"Don't," I say as I raise my hand up to him. I take a step closer to her, so we are standing face to face. My nose is just inches from hers when I say, "Ana. My name is Ana."

"Well, Ana. You need to just get over yourself. It's not like you're his Old Lady or something," Brandie says as she looks back over to Dillon. It's obvious that he's not happy. Anger is written all over his face, and he stares at her with disgust.

"He's mine, Brandi. Now... get... your... fucking hands off him!" I demand as I clench my hands into fists. I've never hit another person, but I really want to punch her in the face... sooo bad.

"I don't see you wearing his name on your back or his ring on your finger," she says bitingly.

"He's mine all the same."

"You've got a lot to learn, little girl," she says as she rolls her eyes. "You're in for a rude awakening. You'll see... you'll never be enough to keep him satisfied."

"Hey, Brandi! My camel called.... He wants his toe back!" Courtney shouts over to Brandi. She's trying to break the tension, but it isn't working. Some of the guys behind her snicker at her remark, so Courtney turns to them and says, "You know what I'm talking about guys!

Brandi's like the first piece of bread in the bag… everyone touches her, but no one wants her." The guys chuckle under their breaths while they shake their heads, but none of them say a word. They know better than to get in the middle of this.

Brandi's face turns beet red with anger as she turns to Courtney and growls, "Fuck off, Courtney."

"I can't help it that your vagina has been used more than Google, Brandi! That's all on you, babe," Courtney says with a sweet smile.

"If you'd just give your men what they need, they wouldn't need me to take up the slack," Brandi snaps back.

"Enough of the bullshit, Brandi. I told you I'm done. Now, back the fuck off. Ana is my Old Lady. Leave her the fuck alone!" Dillon snarls as he stands up and walks over to me, placing his arm around my waist.

"Have fun with that, Sheppard. She looks like she'd be a real blast in the sack. I'll be around when you get tired of playing with Little Miss Perfect," Brandi says flippantly.

"Stop being such a slut bag and just walk away," Courtney snaps at her. "We all know you've been on more wieners than ketchup! It's time for you to take a break."

"Eat shit, Courtney," Brandi growls.

"Did Cindy mention the gift I left in her bed the other night?" Courtney asks with a devilish grin. "Would you like one, too?"

"Stay the fuck out of my room, Courtney!" she demands as she starts to storm off, her high heels clicking across the concrete floor and her hair swaying behind her back. The guys still look extremely amused as she finally walks out of the bar.

"Where the fuck do you come up with that stuff, Court?" Dillon asks.

"What? I was just getting warmed up!" she replies with a big goofy smile.

"Thanks for helping me out, Courtney. I don't know what I was thinking going over there like that," I tell her, already feeling embarrassed for acting like such an ass.

"I liked it," Dillon says as he pulls me closer to him. "I'm going to show you just how much I liked it as soon as we get back to my room."

"I just don't do stuff like that. I don't know what I was thinking!" I explain. "Everyone is going to think I'm a total psychopath or something."

"You were staking your claim, Angel. They get that," he tells me as he kisses me on my forehead.

"Yeah… if you say so," I tell him, unable to even look at him.

"I do. Besides, you're fucking hot when you get all pissed off. Made my dick hard just watching you get all riled up."

"Seriously?" I shout. "I can't believe you just said that!"

"There she is. Love my angry angel," he says as he bends down and places his hands behind my knees, lifting me over his shoulder. Before I can even protest, my ass is up in the air, and my face is at his back. I twist and squirm, trying to free myself as he heads towards his room. I turn my head to the side and see everyone in the bar is watching us, smiling and pointing. My face turns three shades of red when I notice Tessa and the girls sitting at the bar, laughing hysterically. I try to give them my angry face, but end up rolling my eyes and smiling back at them. Something tells me this isn't the first time this sort of thing has happened around here. My attention is drawn back to Dillon when he starts down the hallway.

"Dillon, put me down!" I shout out as I kick my feet back and forth. He reaches up and smacks my ass... hard! "Dillon!!!"

"I've been wanting to do that for weeks, Angel. Better get used to it," he says. My body tingles all over as his threat excites me. I never know what to expect with him, and I love it. The next thing I know, I am being thrown on Dillon's bed as the door slams shut behind us. He stands silent at the edge of the bed, just staring at me with wonder in his eyes.

"Dillon?"

"You're really something, you know that?" he says as he continues to look at me with lust in his eyes.

"Really? I'm a little worried about you, Dillon. I just acted like the biggest neurotic, jealous girlfriend ever, and you liked it."

"I loved it," he says as he leans down to kiss my neck. His warm breath tickles my skin as he whispers, "Liked that you were jealous."

"I was definitely jealous. What do you expect? Brandi's a knock-out."

"She's nothing compared to you, Angel." His lips trail along the edge of my neck to my jaw. "Nothing compares to you. Nothing." I let out a little whimper as he rests his hips between my thighs. "You're all I want, all I need." He looks down at me, his mouth hovering over mine and says, "I love you, Ana." His lips crash down on mine, stealing my breath away.

CHAPTER 15

SHEPPARD

"I NEVER HEARD how things turned out with the Black Diamonds," I tell Bobby.

"Nothing left of them. After you got shot, we took the rest of them out," he tells me as he looks to the floor. "We spent hours looking for you, but…."

"I know, Bobby. It's okay."

"Something in my gut told me you were still alive, so I couldn't give up," Bobby tells me, but he won't look me in the eye. It's still hard for him to talk about it.

"It means a lot to me, brother. I'm sure you would've found me sooner or later," I tell him as I pat him on the shoulder. I can hear the sincerity in his voice as he speaks, and it really does mean a great deal to me.

"I looked it up last night. Did you know that Ana's house is less than two miles away from the Calvert City dock? You were just two miles away from us," Bobby explains. He looks distraught as he thinks back to that day. I hate seeing him like this.

"Listen, Crack Nut. It could have turned out differently, but I'm here now. That's all that matters. I guess it's a good thing Ana decided not to let me die out there in that lake,' I say with a laugh, trying to break the tension in the room.

"We owe her a lot for bringing you back here," Bobby says looking up at me. "You know… Courtney really likes her. She hasn't stopped talking about her."

"Ana likes her, too. She's spent all morning trying to come up with more slut jokes, but none of them are as good as Court's."

"I don't know where she comes up with that shit, but damn… it's funny. The look on Brandi's face… she was so pissed," Bobby says, laughing.

"Do you know what Courtney did to Cindy?" I ask him out of curiosity. Knowing Courtney, there's no telling what she did, but I can guarantee Cindy won't forget it.

"No idea. Believe me… I've tried to find out, but no one's talking," he says as he walks over to his desk. His mood instantly changes when the screen lights up… serious and ready to work. "Did you bring Ana's notes with you?"

"Yeah, but there's not much to them. She's written a few questions down, but she wasn't able to follow up on anything after she was suspended," I say as I hand him the notebook. It's just a thin black medical journal with sporadic notes she'd taken while she was working at the hospital. I just hope Bobby can make some sense of it.

"What reasons did the hospital give for suspending her?" Bobby asks as he starts to flip through the pages of the journal.

"Just a bunch of bullshit. Something about her cheating on some of her old exams, and that she mixed-up some lady's medication, causing her to get sick... and some shit about her having an affair with some married surgeon. None of it was true." Anger surges through me when I think about what they said about her. I'm going to make those fuckers pay for hurting her. Every last one of them.

"Did she take it up with the Hospital Board?" he asks, his eyes still focused on the writing in the journal.

"They denied her request for a hearing. No one would listen to her," I explain. "She's stuck, and the threats against her are only getting worse. There is something to all this."

Bobby quickly scans the pages in the journal, and as he looks through it, he pauses several times to write notes of his own. "This is going to take some time," Bobby tells me.

"Do you think you'll be able to figure this thing out?" I ask him as I look around his room. I have to say that it's a bit intimidating. The guy has every techno gadget known to man. I have no idea what he does with all this stuff, but I do know he's good at what he does. If anybody can find out what's going on, it will be him.

"I don't know yet. I'm going to start with the first three names on her list. There has to be some connection that Ana missed," Bobby says as he starts typing on his computer. "Can you come back in a couple of hours?"

"I'm not going anywhere, Crack Nut. Just tell me

what I can do to help," I tell him. I plan on being here every step of the way until we find a way to help Ana.

"We need to get a folder started for each person on the list, with their names, addresses, medical history, and financial status," he says, pointing over to his other desk.

"I can do that," I say as I get up to collect the folders he was motioning to. I grab several colors, one for each name on the list.

"Once I get into the hospital's network, we can print off each of their records. Their address and phone numbers should be on the forms."

"Maybe Doc can help us with some of the medical stuff," I suggest.

"Good idea. We'll need that once I get everything together." With just a few taps on the keyboard, he has the Grandview Hospital Database pulled up on his computer screen, and he is scanning through all of the pages on the site. I smile to myself as I watch Bobby's knee bouncing like a jack rabbit under his desk. The man is excited. I may have no idea how he does it, but he loves this shit.

"What's the first name on the list?" Bobby asks as he continues to work feverishly, searching through endless pages of information.

I grab the journal and look for the first name. "It's Evelyn McDermott."

The sounds of typing fill the room as he clicks through the site finding everything we might need. "Got it. Go grab those pages off the printer," he tells me.

I walk over to the desk, and I'm surprised by the

amount of paper spouting out into the tray. "What is all this stuff?" I ask.

"Don't know yet. Just put it in the folder," he orders.

Once I've placed the enormous stack of paper into the folder, he asks for the second and third name. Each person ends up with large pile of papers added to their folder. I flip through the pages, and it all looks like a foreign language to me.

"We need to see if there are any irregularities in their medical treatment. See if you can get Ana and Doc in here to start sorting through all that paperwork," Bobby tells me.

I nod and head out to find them.

When I walk into the kitchen, Ana is standing there with John Warren sitting on her hip. He has a strand of her blonde hair in one hand and a cookie in the other. She's whispering something to him, but I can't make out what she's saying. Her facial expressions are just too damn cute. I want to stand here and watch her, but Bobby is waiting.

"Ana?" I call out to her. She turns to face me, and her face lights up with a bright smile when she sees me standing there.

"Hey, babe," she answers as she brushes the cookie crumbs off John Warren's shirt. "We're just having a snack. Lily asked me to watch him while she did inventory."

"You look good holding him like that," I tell her.

Her cheeks turn a light shade of pink as she looks down at John Warren. "I like hanging out with him. He's such a sweet baby."

"I want kids, Angel. Lots of them… soon."

"Umm… okay… I want that, too. Is that what you came in here to tell me?" she asks in surprise.

"Bobby's got some stuff for you to look over," I explain.

A serious look crosses her face before she says, "I'll be right there. Let me take JW back to Lily first." She takes his sippy cup off of the counter and starts walking towards me. "He's so cute. I could spend hours playing with him."

"Let's get this shit sorted, Angel. Then you can spend all the time you want with him, and we can talk about starting a family of our own," I tell her, owning her with my eyes as I lean down and kiss her on her forehead.

"I'd like that," she says, leaning into me and smiling. "Give me five minutes, and I'll meet you in Bobby's room."

"I'm going to get Doc. Maybe he can help."

"Good idea," she says before she walks out.

We all meet back in Bobby's room, and Ana and Doc start going through the first folder. Ana spreads out the papers all over Bobby's bed as she frantically reads each and every page, searching for anything that might help us end this.

"So this Evelyn McDermott… was she the first patient you were concerned about?" Doc asks Ana.

"Yes. When we were doing rounds, I noticed that they were running several unnecessary tests on her. I asked Jason about it, but he just blew me off. I even asked the Chief of Staff. He told me to tend to my own patients and leave it alone."

"What kind of tests?" Bobby asks.

"Some of them were just routine checks for her scheduled hysterectomy... urinalysis, an ultrasound, basic blood work. But the tissue sample... that's what caught my attention. There was just no need for tissue type for a basic hysterectomy. She had no signs of cancer, or any other irregularities, so I didn't see the need for it."

"Tissue type?" I ask. She's talking over my head with all this medical stuff, but I hate to slow her down by asking a bunch of trivial questions.

"It's used to match the number of antigens that an organ donor has with the recipient share."

"English, babe. No idea what you're talking about."

"The antigens recognize the differences between two people's body tissues. They are like markers... they help tell which donor is the best match. For a successful transplant, you need six out of six matches," she explains.

"I think she's on to something here," Doc says. "These guys are definitely up to something... something big."

Ana and Doc make a list of all the testing done on the patients that she had in her journal. Doc pushes up his reading glasses as he sorts through his stack of papers and asks Ana, "Did you see this?" He hands her a piece of paper and says, "Looks like Evelyn's family requested an autopsy. It's dated around the time you were suspended."

"Damn..." Ana whispers as she looks at the sheet of paper. "Do you see the actual autopsy?"

"No... I don't see it," Doc tells her as he flips through his stack of papers. "Bobby, can you check the pathology department? See if they have any record of it there."

"On it," Bobby says as he turns back to his computer.

CHAPTER 16

ANA

IT'S OFFICIAL... I have a migraine, the migraine to end all migraines. I could feel it creeping up on me when we were going through all that paperwork, but I didn't think it would get this bad. I finally had to leave it for a little while and come lay down in Dillon's bed. I should feel relieved; for the first time, someone is really listening to me, but I don't. Instead, it's like all of my worries and doubts are being confirmed... one by one. I just don't know where it's all going to end.

I need to talk to my dad... just hear his voice for a minute, so I roll over and grab my phone.

"Hey, Dad."

"Hey there, sweetheart. I've been wondering when I was going to hear from you. How are things going?" he asks.

"They're good... really good," I say, trying to mask the fact that I am freaking out.

"That doesn't sound very convincing, Ana. What's going on?" he asks.

"It's nothing. We're just going through some of the

stuff from the hospital. I got a little overwhelmed and had to get away from it all for a minute," I tell him.

"It will all work out, honey. You just have to be patient. Don't get too worked up and get one of those damn headaches of yours." I smile, thinking how he knows me too well.

"Okay, Daddy. I'll do my best," I tell him. "How's Steven today?"

"He's actually coming around. He'll be in the hospital for a few more days, but I think he'll be okay."

"Did you tell him why I'm not there?" I ask. I roll over on my side and try to use my arm to shield my eyes. The light coming through the blinds is excruciating, making my headache worse.

"He understands, Ana. He just wants you to be safe," he tells me. "That's what we both want. Hopefully, Dillon knows what he's up against. Tell him to call me if he needs anything."

"I will, and keep me posted on Steven. Tell him I asked about him."

"I will. You do the same."

"Okay… I love you, Daddy." I miss him… more than I'd realized.

"I love you too, sweetheart. Talk to you soon," he says just before he hangs up the phone. Tears instantly fill my eyes. I hate feeling sorry for myself, but these headaches bring it out in me. I close my eyes and try to block out all the crazy thoughts racing through my head. After a few minutes, I finally manage to fall asleep.

Some noise down the hall startles me, waking me up

from my deep sleep. I slowly open my eyes, and I am relieved that my headache has finally gone away. I smile when I realize Dillon's warm body is pressed against my side, the heat of his breath on my neck. The slow and steady rhythm of his breathing almost draws me back to sleep, but having him so close is too much of a distraction. I can't resist him. I need to see him, to touch him. I run my fingers along the lines of his fingers, memorizing every ridge and callous. I find myself becoming aroused with this simple touch, bringing a mischievous thought to my mind.

I ease his hand off my hip and lower it down at his side. When I start to move, he lets out a deep breath and rolls over on his back. I freeze, hoping he won't open his eyes. The tension alone excites me. After a few seconds, I ease up on my side, being careful not to move the bed too much. I inch my way down the contour of his body until I'm at the perfect spot and begin undoing the buttons of his fly… five copper buttons, each one more alluring than the last. I take a deep breath as I see more and more of his bulge. I begin to slowly slide his jeans down his hips, inch by inch as I watch for any signs that he may be waking up. I smile with excitement and satisfaction when I finally have them down below his waist.

"That'll do," I whisper to myself. I take a minute to just look at him, lying there on display. He's perfect. All of him. My body feels like it's virtually on fire as I think of having him in my mouth. It has me both curious and scared out of my mind, but it seems natural… I want to do this. I want to please and pleasure him, but the thought of hurting him or doing something wrong almost stops me. I release my fears, and my mouth begins to water as I let my fingers trail along the smooth skin, exploring every inch of him. His breathing begins to change slightly when I take him in my hand, gently moving up and down his shaft. I look up at his handsome face, checking to see if he is waking up. When I see that he's still sleeping, I lower my mouth down to his cock and gently press my tongue against his flesh. My heart begins to race as I twirl it around the head. The round metal ball of his piercing rakes across the roof of my mouth, reminding me what it feels like to have him inside me. It's like nothing I've ever felt before… it's intoxicating. When I take him in my mouth, the faint taste of salt trickles across my taste buds, but there's something more… an underlying flavor that's all him, making me crave more. I continue to move my hand along his shaft as I take him farther into my mouth, sucking as I take him deeper into my throat. His cock is steadily growing more erect, thrilling me as I try to keep my rhythm steady.

"Ana?" Dillon mumbles, but I don't stop. I look up at him as I brush my tongue along the head of his dick and down to the base. His eyes are filled with lust as he watches me, burning me with desire. I love how his body responds to my touch. His fingers dive into my hair, guiding me as I find the rhythm that he wants. I am lost in the moment, when his body tenses.

"Teeth, babe," he warns.

I stop moving, hating the thought that I might have hurt him. I pull back, frozen with doubt.

"Don't you dare fucking stop, Angel." I pause for another brief second, but ultimately decide to keep going. I cautiously lower my mouth back down over him as I tighten my grasp at the base of his cock. I ease my way back and forth, trying to be careful as I follow his guided pace. He lets out a deep moan, encouraging me… fueling me to keep going. His hips rise up from the bed, driving him farther into my mouth. A deep growl vibrates through his chest as I flick my tongue against his piercing. I feel a sense of pride knowing that I am learning what he likes. I want to please him, to make him remember the feel of my mouth against his skin. I'm beginning to realize why so many women enjoy doing this. There is such a sense of power knowing that I can affect him this way with just my touch.

His breathing begins to quicken, his chest rising and falling with increased intensity. I slowly begin to twist my wrist as I move my hand up and down his shaft, taking him deep into my throat. His cock throbs against my tongue, growing harder every second.

"Angel… I'm going to cum," he warns. I moan with pleasure, feeling a sense of gratification that I've brought him to the edge of his release. His balls grow hard and tight, while his cock throbs against my fingers. I continue moving up and down his shaft as I pull him farther into my mouth, twirling my tongue along his hard cock. His breathing stops and the muscles in his body become rigid. I feel him begin to swell and get even harder in my mouth. His moans echo through the room as I increase my pace. His hips thrust forward, letting me know he's about to cum. His cock begins convulsing against my tongue as he erupts in my mouth, shooting hot spurts down my throat. A sense of satisfaction takes over as I swallow what he has given me, loving the taste of him against my tongue… bitter, yet sweet.

"Fuck," he grunts as I continue to lick him clean.

"Don't know what brought that on, but that was fucking fantastic," he says with a low husky voice. A sexy smile crosses his face, as he reaches out for me and pulls me back into his arms, his cock still resting outside of his pants.

I let out a deep sigh as I look down at his waist. He shakes his head and says, "You're going to have to give me a minute."

I run my fingers over the lines of one of his tattoos and ask, "Was it okay? I mean… really?" I was feeling pretty confident earlier, but now I'm feeling a little insecure.

"Absolutely. Love having your mouth on my dick." His hand reaches for my face, lifting my chin so I'm looking into his eyes. "I hope you liked it, because you're going to be doing that again. Often. Like on a daily basis."

I can't help but laugh. He always knows how to make me feel so at ease, "I love you, Dillon."

His blue eyes pierce through me as it sinks in. I hadn't realized that this was the first time I'd actually said the words. "Say it again."

"I love you."

"All of it, Angel."

"I love you, Dillon," I say as I lower my head onto his chest, my fingers still trailing his ink.

"You're mine, Angel. Now and forever," he whispers as he kisses me on my temple. We lay there for several minutes, just enjoying the feel of our bodies lying close to one another. I love how he makes me feel so safe, like the world around me isn't really spinning out of control.

We are pulled from our thoughts when there is a loud knock on Dillon's door.

"Got something you both need to see," Bobby shouts through the door. "Meet me at the bar. I need a beer... maybe two."

"Be there in a minute," Dillon tells him as he tugs his pants up over his hips. "Let's go see what he's found out," he says as he gets up out of the bed. He puts his hand out to me and helps me up. "We're going to fix this thing, Angel. You're going to have everything you've ever wanted. I promise you that."

It means so much to me that Dillon is trying to help me like this. Being a doctor has been a dream of mine for as long as I can remember, but it just doesn't seem like the most important thing anymore. Just having my life back will be enough. A chance to have a future with the man that I love... that's all I really need.

CHAPTER 17

SHEPPARD

When Ana and I walk in, Bobby and Doc are sitting at the bar. Bobby is drinking a beer as he studies the piece of paper he's holding. He's mumbling something to Doc, but stops when he sees us walk up. I grab a couple of beers from the cooler and sit down beside them.

"We got the autopsy report," Bobby says as he hands her the sheet of paper. "Something's not right."

Doc walks over to the end of the counter where Ana is sitting as he says, "She had a pretty severe case of endometriosis, which is why they decided to do a hysterectomy. But her records show that she had a complete workup done, and all her labs came back normal." He takes a long pull off of his beer and continues, "She was physically fit, and showed no signs of cancer."

"I know all of that, Doc," Ana sighs with a look of frustration. I hand her a beer, and she takes a quick drink before saying, "Is there anything else?"

"The autopsy results show that she had a kidney

removed. The medical report said it was cancerous, and that they had no option other than to take it out," Bobby explains.

Ana eyes widen as she looks over the report. Her head shakes back and forth as she tries to make sense of it all. "This can't be right."

"That's what they're saying," Bobby tells her as he hands her Evelyn's folder.

She immediately takes out one of the pages and looks it over before she turns to Doc. "Look. I just can't believe this. It says it right here! The lab tests came back completely normal," she says as she jabs the piece of paper in her hand. "They even did a twenty-four hour urine collection, and it showed no signs of any irregularities."

"We know, Ana," Doc tells her calmly. "That's what we're trying to tell you. The facts just don't add up. There has to be another reason they removed her kidney."

It is like a light turns on in her head and everything becomes clear. Her eyes widen, and a look of panic crosses her face. "Shit… Shit… Shit!!! The tissue sampling! Oh my God… they just took it!! They stole her kidney!" Ana screeches.

"That's what we're thinking," Bobby says. "It would explain why they freaked out when you started asking questions. Then, when Evelyn's family began to look into things, they blamed you. They needed to get you out of the way, so that they could continue on with their plan."

"Do you think they tried to kill her?" Ana asks.

"No. The hysterectomy was the perfect cover up. The recovery time would have been almost the same. No one would've suspected anything," Doc explains.

"I don't understand. Why would they do this?" Ana asks.

"Why else? Money," I tell her as I finish off my beer.

"This whole thing is crazy! We're talking about a small town hospital. How could they ever pull this off without everyone finding out?" Ana asks with a bewildered look frozen on her face.

"Really it's the perfect setup. Jason's family basically owns the hospital. They have full control of everything that happens there. And because it's a small hospital, no one would ever suspect a thing," Bobby tells her.

"Are there others?" Ana asks. It's killing me to see her upset. Watching all of this unfold before our eyes is pretty fucking unbelievable for everyone, though.

"Yes, but it looks like things have slowed down since Evelyn died. I went through pathology and checked to see how often they've done tissue sampling over the past year. In the past six months, there have been at least nine, maybe ten," Bobby tells her.

"Ten!" Ana cries with a horrified look on her face. "How are they getting away with this?"

"All of the patients have been through some kind of invasive surgery, and as soon as the doctors mention cancer, people just believe them. We all know that everyone gets freaked out by just the mention of cancer. There's no surprise that they didn't suspect foul play.

These doctors were able to take a kidney or part of a liver without the patients ever questioning it. It was all working out for them until Evelyn died," Bobby explains.

"We need to find out who else is involved," Doc says to Ana.

"What do you mean?" I ask.

"These patients have to be referred to Jason or his dad by someone. We need to find out who it is," he clarifies.

This shit is fucked up. I knew it was going to be bad, but I had no idea it was going to be this insane. I grab another beer and start guzzling it down. Just thinking about what these motherfuckers are doing makes my head spin. No wonder they're after Ana. They thought she knew more than she actually did. She's the one person that could expose them, and there was no way they were going to take that risk.

"This thing… Dillon, we have to stop them." Ana looks over to me and pleads. "Please… we have to do something." Her face is filled with anguish. She leans in, resting her body against mine. I like that she finds comfort in me, knowing I'll do whatever it takes to make things right.

I wrap my arm around her waist and pull her closer to me as I tell her, "We will, Angel. You have my word on that."

"Thank you," she says as a tear falls down her cheek.

I kiss her on her forehead before I turn to Bobby and ask, "What do we have on Jason and his dad?"

"Gonna work on them next," he says as he reaches for another beer. "It won't take me long to get what I need."

"Sounds good, Crack Nut," I tell him.

We spend a few minutes talking about the garage and some of the new bikes Bishop has coming in. I'm looking forward to getting back to work. I've missed it. Doc is bragging about his latest remodel when Brandi and Cindy walk into the bar.

As soon as they see Maverick's brother, Gavin, sitting in the corner, they stop in their tracks and stare at him. He smiles as he pats the empty spot on the sofa, calling them over. They instantly start walking over to him. He raises his beer towards me, and I give him a chin lift in appreciation for keeping the girls distracted.

At first, I was surprised to see that Maverick's brother is here prospecting with us, but he's turned out to be a pretty good addition to the club so far. When I asked him why he wasn't prospecting with Maverick's club, all he said was that he needed a change. I didn't push. Club life seems natural for him, and so far he's proven himself to be useful. The girls jump at his invitation, practically running to the sofa. They immediately begin trying their magic on him.

"Who's that?" Ana asks.

"Gavin. He's one of our new prospects," Bobby tells her.

"He's got his hands full with them," she says, laughing.

"No doubt about that," Doc tells her as he shakes

his head.

It doesn't take long before they start making a scene, and Bobby takes it as a sign that it's time to wrap things up. "I'm starving. What's for dinner?"

"No idea, but we need to find out," Doc tells him. "I'm ready to eat."

"I'm really not hungry," Ana chimes in.

"Ana," I warn. "You've gotta eat. I don't want that headache coming back," I tell her as I brush a loose strand of hair behind her ear. I lean down with my mouth close to her and whisper, "I've got plans for you tonight, Angel. It's my turn to have a little fun." I say it as I lick the outline of her ear. Her eyes brighten with mischief, and I can't hold back my smile. My angel likes to play. I like that. No… I fucking love that.

CHAPTER 18

ANA

"BOBBY IS AMAZING," I tell Courtney. "How did he learn to do all that stuff?"

"I really don't know. He says it just comes naturally to him. He tries to make it out like it's no big deal, but I know he's special… in more ways than he knows," she says as she looks over to him at the other end of the table. He's engrossed in a conversation with Bishop and Dillon, obviously sharing everything we found out earlier. Since Dillon decided it was time for us all to have something to eat, we're sitting waiting on Levi and Connor to bring in our dinner. They're still prospecting for the club, so they have to do all the stuff no one else wants to do. I don't really understand it, but Dillon says it's a rite of passage. He says they served in the military with him, and they're used to all the grunt work. They've been outside with Gavin cooking burgers for the past half hour. I guess Dillon was right about me needing to eat something, because the smell from the grill is making me a little hungry.

"So… when are y'all going to get married?" I ask

Courtney.

"Soon, I guess. He wants to elope like Goliath and Lily, but I want a wedding… a real wedding, with the fancy dress and all my friends and family."

"I love weddings. There's just something about watching two people in love taking that next step. It's all just so romantic," I tell her.

The back door flies open, and Connor walks in carrying a huge tray of burgers and hot dogs, the smell of burning charcoal still lingering on his clothes. My stomach is in full overdrive by the time he sets the tray on the table.

"That's what I'm talking about," Bull shouts as he begins to fill his plate with food. Within seconds, his plate is stacked high, and he is taking his first bite.

"Hungry?" Doc asks sarcastically.

It doesn't take long for all the food to disappear from the table. We were all hungry, and it was nice to have something to take our minds off of everything, even if it was only for a little while.

"We need to see if we know anyone on the State Medical Board. It's time to let them know what's going on," Bishop tells Dillon.

"I'll look into it," Doc says. "I may know someone that can help us out."

"I want them to pay for what they've done to Ana… and all the people they've hurt," Dillon snaps.

"They'll pay," Bishop assures him. "You can count on it."

"I'll work on Jason and his dad tonight. See what I

can find on them. We need to find out who they're working with," Bobby tells them.

"The referring doctor's name should be on their records. It shouldn't be hard to find," I tell them.

"I'll get it all. Just going to take some time," Bobby says.

"Well, maybe Ana would like to hang with me while you guys do your recon." Courtney turns to me and asks, "Wanna watch a movie or something and get your mind off things for a bit?"

I look over to Dillon, wondering if he's okay with me leaving. He smiles and says, "You should go, Angel."

"Okay… if you're sure you don't need me to stay and help," I say, not feeling exactly comfortable leaving them all to take care of this on their own. It doesn't feel right asking them to work on this without me.

"Go, babe. You need a break," he tells me. "But I'm sending Levi and Connor with you."

"Oh! We can go see the Lazarus Effect or Insurgent… maybe both!" Courtney says excitedly.

"Okay," I tell her. I get up and put my now empty paper plate in the garbage.

"Give me a second to grab my purse, and I'll meet you out front," Courtney calls back to me as she walks out of the kitchen. "And tell Connor he's buying the popcorn!"

Dillon walks over to me and says, "Go have a good time."

"Are you sure about this?" I ask.

"I'm sure, Ana. We're going to take care of this.

We'll burn them to the ground… leave nothing but ashes when we're done," he says, reassuring me.

"Thank you," I tell him. "Thank you for everything."

His hands reach up, his palms resting on the sides of my face, and he says, "I told you, Angel… I take care of what's mine. Trust me to take care of this." He pulls me closer, pressing his lips against mine. The kiss isn't long, but it's enough… just enough to comfort me, making me believe that everything really is going to be okay.

CHAPTER 19

SHEPPARD

"THEY WERE ALL referred by a general practitioner named Dr. Samuel Harris," Bobby tells me as he scrolls through the pages on his computer screen. "He has a small practice in Calvert City."

Bobby's been working on this shit for hours, and the stacks of papers just keep growing. I just hope there's enough evidence to end this thing.

"Did you find anything on Jason or his dad?" I ask.

"His dad's computer is clear. Looks like Jason does all the grunt work. He searches the donor list, looking for patients that have waited the longest for their transplant, and he looks into their financial records. He contacts those that would be desperate enough to pay for a transplant… without asking questions."

"What's next?" I ask.

"Doc's friend is making an inquiry to the Kentucky State Medical Board letting them know we need to speak to them," Bobby starts. "Now we have to wait to see what they say."

"How long do you think that will take?" I ask.

"Maybe an hour... maybe a week. No way to be sure," he replies.

"Are you done for the night?"

"Yeah... until we hear back from them, there's not much else we can do," Bobby says.

"Thanks, Crack Nut. I really appreciate all this."

"No need to thank me. It's the least I can do for Ana for saving your life," he says, smiling. I start for the door before he calls, "Shep?"

"Yeah?"

"There's a good chance that someone at the Medical Board will contact Jason or his dad. You might want to keep your eyes on Ana at all times, until this thing blows over... just to be on the safe side."

"Will do, brother. Let me know if you hear anything," I tell him as I walk out of his room and head back to mine. I need to find Ana and see for myself that she is okay. After hearing Bobby's warning, a sudden claw of fear is choking at me... I have to keep her close, protect her at all costs.

When I walk into my room, she's standing with her back to me. She's just gotten out of the shower. Her hair is wet, falling loose around her shoulders, and she's wearing her bathrobe. Her scent fills the room, fresh and clean like soap. I inhale deeply, releasing the tension I felt earlier. Just being in the same room with her eases the heavy thoughts that constantly race through my mind. I'm in love with her. I never thought I would feel this way about a woman, but now I've never wanted anything more. She's mine, and I want a future with her.

When this thing with the hospital is done, I want to be able to take her home… to our home. I told her I would give her everything she has ever wanted, and I'm going to do everything in my power to make that happen.

She turns around with her bathrobe slightly draped open, revealing a glimpse of her beautiful, naked body. Instantly, my cock is hard as granite. I need to be inside her. She stands still as I make my way over to her, my eyes never leaving hers. My hands slip inside her robe, caressing her soft skin. I begin kissing her neck as I slide the bathrobe off her body, letting it drop to the floor. Without removing my mouth from her neck, I slowly guide her to the wall behind her.

"Turn around, Angel. Palms against the wall," I tell her firmly. Her eyes sparkle with excitement as she follows my command. "Don't move. Keep your hands flat against the wall."

My eyes roam over her body, devouring the perfect curve of her ass. When I step closer, she begins to wiggle that sweet little naked ass against my cock. Slowly, I slide my hand down to her pussy and press my fingers against her clit, rubbing it in slow and steady circles. Within seconds, she's soaking wet grinding her bare ass against my dick.

"More, Dillon…" she whispers softly. "Play with me like you promised earlier."

"Is that what you want, baby?" I ask as I continue stroking her clit. With my free hand, I quickly unfasten my jeans and let them fall to the floor.

"Spread your legs," I tell her as I guide her hips out

to meet mine. I slide my cock between her legs and graze her clit with the head of my dick. Her hips thrust back against me as she moans out in frustration. Reaching up, I grab her hands and move them over her head. Without saying a word, she peeks over her shoulder, giving me that mischievous smile I love. I slide my cock along her opening and squeeze her ass as she begins to beg. When I continue taunting her, she drops her head and lets out a deep breath.

"Please… I need you," she pleads as she begins to move her body, her hands shifting slightly from the wall.

"Hands, Ana."

She quickly places them back above her head and waits eagerly for my cock. I run my tongue along the curve of her neck as my fingers dig into her hips.

"Are you ready for me, Angel? Do you want my cock?" I whisper in her ear.

"Yes, Dillon… please!"

"That's my girl," I tell her just before I slam into her. As soon as I feel her clamping onto my cock with a vise hold, I know this is gonna be fast. Her back arches as I begin pounding into her flesh, each thrust harder and deeper than before. I reach my hand around to her pussy, rotating between circling, pinching and rubbing it, just how she likes. The need to get her there with me possesses me. I'm close to my release when her body begins to tense and her breathing becomes ragged and forced. I increase my rhythm, forcing her over the edge. She cries out my name as her pussy clamps down on my cock, urging me to find my release. I finally let myself go.

"Fuck," I growl loudly. My body jerks and jolts as I cum inside her.

She looks back over her shoulder and smiles before she gasps, "That was…."

"Incredible," I finish as I lift her up and carry her over to the bed. As soon as our bodies fall to the bed, she curls into my side, resting her head on my shoulder.

"I love you, Dillon," she whispers.

"I love you, too, Angel," I tell her as I kiss her temple. After a few moments, her breathing becomes slow and steady, letting me know she's fallen asleep. I listen to her for a few minutes longer before I finally crash from exhaustion. We've been asleep for several hours when Ana's phone begins to ring. I try to just ignore it, but the annoying beeps of a text message keep me from falling back to sleep.

"Can you hand me my phone?" Ana asks. Apparently it woke her up, too. "It might be my dad."

I reach over to get it off the nightstand and hand it to her. She stretches and lets out the cutest damn yawn before she brings the phone closer to her face. Her eyes widen as she looks at the screen. She quickly sits up on the bed and shouts, "Oh my God! They got Steven!"

I grab the phone from her hands and focus on the picture of Steven on the screen. His body lays lifeless on a gurney with his eyes closed and his clothes removed. I scroll through several pictures before I finally come across a message:

You should have left it alone. Disappear and keep your mouth closed or YOU'RE NEXT!

"They're going to kill him," Ana says frantically, tears flowing down her face. There's no doubt they're up to something, and I have to try to stop them.

"Call your dad," I tell her. "Tell him to get over to the hospital now."

"My dad? I'm scared... what if they try to hurt him, too, Dillon?" she cries.

"Tell him not to go alone. Ask him to take one of his farmhands with him in case there's any trouble," I tell her as I hand her the phone.

She immediately calls her father. Her voice quivers as she tries to tell him what is going on. When she starts to cry again, I take the phone and say, "Go to the hospital first, but don't go alone. Call me as soon as you find out anything. I'm on my way."

As soon as he hangs up the phone, I get up and start getting dressed. "I need to see Bishop before I go."

"I want to go with you," she pleads.

"Not happening, Ana. I need you to stay here where I know you'll be safe," I tell her.

"What are you going to do?" she asks.

"I'm going to take care of this," I tell her. I have no idea how it will play out, but I do know one thing... this ends tonight.

CHAPTER 20

ANA

I HATE THIS. Watching Dillon leave with Renegade and Goliath was almost unbearable. I wanted to go with them, try to do something to help, but Dillon wouldn't hear of it. He wanted me to stay here where he knows no one can get to me. I know he's right, but I'm miserable. How am I supposed to just sit here and wait, not knowing what is really happening?

I get back in the bed, and I can't fight back my tears. I'm scared out of my mind. I know I need to try and go back to sleep, but my mind is reeling. I can't get the pictures of Steven out of my head. He looked so vulnerable lying there, totally unaware of what they were doing to him. My imagination is running wild, wondering what exactly they could be doing to him. In my gut, I know what that text means, I'll never see Steven again. I just can't bear it, and I know it's all my fault. I should've tried harder. I knew things were off. If I had figured this all out on my own, none of this would have happened. I toss and turn, trying to block it from my thoughts, but it's useless. Not knowing what's going on is the hardest part. I just need to know if Dillon's okay.

There's a light tap on the door before Tessa walks into the room. She walks over and sits on the edge of the bed. "How are you making it?" she asks as she tightens the belt on her bathrobe.

"I'm freaking out," I tell her as I sit up in the bed. "I can't stop thinking about it. Do you think they will be okay?"

"I do, Ana. I really do. Sheppard is one of the best men I know. He knows how to handle himself, and I know he will do whatever it takes to make this right. Goliath and Renegade are with him. They'll make sure nothing happens to him," she says, trying to reassure me.

"This is all my fault," I tell her. "I should've tried...."

"No, Ana. None of this is your fault. Bishop told me what those people are doing, and they have to be stopped," she says with a pained look on her face. I know what she is saying is true, but I still feel so guilty.

"What if..." I start.

"I know it's hard, but you're going to have to trust Sheppard. He'll make this right."

"I just don't want him to get hurt. I don't think I could survive it if something happened to him," I explain. Just the thought of something happening to him brings tears to my eyes. I love him so much and just want him to come back to me.

"I've been where you are now... more times than I like to admit. I'd like to say that it gets easier, but it doesn't. I always worry about him, but he's never failed to make it out okay," she says as she reaches over and squeezes my hand. "They're good at this, honey. You just have to be patient and try to have a little faith."

"Okay… I'll try." I know what she's saying is right, but it's hard not to worry.

"In a few days, this will all be behind us, and you can concentrate on your future with Shep. Do you want to finish your residency?" she asks.

"I don't know… I just don't think I can go back there, especially after everything that's happened," I explain. "It's just too much."

"Can't you do it at another hospital? Maybe you can do it here," she offers.

"I'd have to see if I can get my suspension cleared, but yeah… being a doctor has always been a dream of mine, and I really want a chance to finish what I started. I'd really like to try to do it here… with Dillon."

"Doc knows several of the doctors here. I'm sure he can help you get on if you decide that's something you might like to do."

"Really? I'd love that. It would mean a lot to me."

"Great! I'll talk to him in the morning. Let's see if there's something he can do," she tells me.

"Thanks, Tessa. I really appreciate everything you and Bishop have done for me."

"Ana, you don't have to thank me. You brought Sheppard back to us, and it's obvious that he's crazy about you. We want to do whatever we can to help," she says as she stands up. "Try to get some rest. I'll come by in the morning to check on you."

"That's easier said than done, but I'll try," I tell her

as I lay back down.

As soon as she leaves the room, my anxiety starts to set in again. I can't help but worry about Dillon. I try to focus on everything that Tessa just told me, but my heart sinks when I think of all the horrible things that could happen. I just want this thing to be over, so Dillon can come back to me… now.

CHAPTER 21

SHEPPARD

WE'D BEEN DRIVING for over an hour when I got the call from Ana's dad. He'd done like I asked and taken his best farmhand with him to look for Steven at the hospital. When they got there, he was gone. When he asked where Steven was, one of the nurses told him that he'd just been released, and someone had already taken him home. He wasn't supposed to be released for several more days, so they rushed back to Steven's in hopes that they'd missed him.

When he pulled onto their street, he knew something was wrong. His voice shook with anger as he told me about the firetrucks speeding past him as he made his way up to Steven's house. The fire and smoke billowed into the dark sky as firemen swarmed around trying to put out the blaze, but there was no use. It was burning out of control, and there was little they could do to stop it. When he tried to approach the house, they blocked him, telling him it was for his own safety. They told him there had been some kind of explosion. They blamed it on a gas leak, but he knew that wasn't what happened.

I could tell from his voice that he was devastated. He blamed himself for not keeping a better eye on him and making sure Steven was safe. I tried to convince him that there was nothing he could've done, but he wouldn't listen. Steven was like a son to him, and he thought he let him down.

Once I hung up the phone with Ana's dad, I knew it was time to pay Jason a visit. There wasn't anything we could do for Steven now, but we could stop these motherfuckers before they got to Ana or hurt anyone else. I told Goliath and Renegade about the fire, and I followed them down the Interstate. I was thankful to be on my bike instead of in a cage tonight. Listening to the rumble of the engine is the best way for me to clear my head, and I need that more than ever.

When we pull onto Jason's road, we kill our engines. It's after three in the morning, and we don't want to risk being heard. Everything is quiet when we pull our bikes behind his house. I look over to Goliath and Renegade as they get off their bikes and immediately feel a sense of gratitude. They are my brothers… always there when I need them. They both look to me and nod, letting me know they're ready to go.

As we approach his back door, we realize the asshole doesn't even have a fucking alarm system. Renegade and I stand watch while Goliath works his magic on the lock. When it pops open, a sly smile slowly spreads across his face. The man loves this shit. I shake my head, laughing to myself as he gestures for us to go inside first.

My adrenaline is on overdrive as we make our way

into the house. When we get inside, everything is pitch black. It's difficult to see, but the floor plan is simple. We have no problem knowing where we are going. Goliath and Renegade follow me down the small hallway that leads to the back bedrooms. Our heavy boots cause the floors to creak and pop as we make our way into his room, adding tension to every step we take. I can't believe the noise doesn't wake him, but sure enough, there he sleeps all curled up in his bed. His breathing is heavy and deep, and I smile thinking how surprised the motherfucker is going to be when he wakes up.

Excitement rushes through my veins as I stand there staring at him from the edge of the bed, waiting for Goliath to give me the go ahead. I grab one of the pillows lying beside his head and press it against his face, blocking all the oxygen from his lungs. His body instantly begins to thrash and jerk, trying to break free from my hold. His hands frantically grab and pull at my arms, trying to wrench the pillow from his face. Goliath grabs his feet, preventing him from falling off of the bed.

It doesn't take long for Jason's body to begin to become limp, letting me know it is time to take the pillow off his face. He gasps and coughs as he tries to pull the air back into his lungs. I lower my face close to his and say, "Good morning, sunshine."

"What the fuck?" he sputters.

Before he has a chance to say anything else, my fist connects with his chin. His eyes roll back, and his body falls completely limp. Motherfucker is knocked out cold. Goliath takes his hands and secures them over his head, while Renegade and I tie his feet to the footboard of the bed. I go into the kitchen and after I fill a pitcher full of water, I head back into the bedroom. I stand over him and slowly begin to pour it over his face.

He starts to shake his head from side to side as he tries to avoid the cascading water. "It's time to wake up, motherfucker."

He pulls at his restraints as he spits the water out of his mouth and shouts, "What do you want?" The bedpost clanks against the wall as he pulls at the ropes binding his hands. He looks over to me and asks, "Why are you doing this?"

"You've been a busy man, Jason… very busy," I tell him. "Tell me about Steven."

"I don't know what you're talking about! I don't know anything…" he starts, but he stops when he sees the knife I'm holding in my hand. I lower it to his chest and use it to cut a line down the middle of his t-shirt.

"And Evelyn? I guess you don't know anything about her either," I say as I press the edge of the blade against his hip, close to his kidney.

"I… uh… oh god, please don't kill me!" he pleads, pulling frantically at the ropes.

"I want you to listen to me, Jason," I tell him as the blade begins to cut into his skin. It isn't deep, but it is enough to cause blood to trickle down his side. "I want you to listen… very… carefully."

"Please!" he begs as he looks down at the blood staining his sheets.

"You're going to tell me everything you know…

about Ana… those patients at the hospital… and Steven." I drag the blade over to the other side of his chest, scratching the first few layers of his skin. I press deeper into his other hip, causing the blood to begin to flow as I say, "And don't leave out anything, motherfucker."

"Ana?" he asks, squirming beneath my knife. "Fuck me… that bitch just keeps causing problems. Should've taken care of her weeks ago."

Rage surges through me, and I jab the knife deep into his side. He grunts in agony when I pull the knife free. "Watch your fucking mouth," I shout. "Or I'll end you right now!"

"Just do it, asshole! You're going to kill me anyway… just get it over with!"

Goliath steps closer to the bed and says, "When we leave here, we're going to go see your parents… I'm sure your mother…."

"No! Please don't!! She didn't have anything to do with any of this," he shouts. "It was my father. It was all his idea. I… I just helped him. And… and when Ana started asking questions, he told me to take care of it."

"Is that why you had her suspended?" I ask.

"That's her fault! As soon as she started snooping, I did everything I could to get her to leave. I thought it was enough to get her to give up and move on… try to get on at another hospital, but she wouldn't give it up. When she wouldn't leave, my father had her suspended," Jason explains.

"We know about the transplants," Goliath says as he

leans over him. "Maybe you'd like to be added to the donor list.... I'm sure that you're a perfect match for someone out there."

"I'm sorry! But if Ana had just kept her damn mouth shut, nothing would have happened to her."

"Tell me about Steven," I demand.

"When Dad got a message from the Medical Board tonight, we both knew Ana was behind it. She didn't leave me any choice. I had to shut her up and make her disappear," Jason admits. "I sedated him, and after I took a few pictures, I took him to his house and set the fire. It's all her fault. The cunt should've kept her damn...."

"Motherfucker," I yell as I begin my assault on his face. "Her name is Ana!" My fist crashes into his face again and again. "You are never to speak of her again. Ever! As of this moment, she is forgotten, along with us. We were never fucking here. If you run your mouth, I'll finish what I started, and I won't stop with you." My knuckles sting from the continuous blows I pound into his face in rhythm with the message I'm giving him, but I don't stop. It isn't until after I've knocked out his front teeth that Goliath pulls me off of him.

"Rein it in, brother. Remember what Bishop said... we don't need him dead. They'll be here any minute," Goliath warns. I look down at his bloody face, almost unrecognizable from all of the swelling and bruising.

Renegade sits down at Jason's desk and turns on his computer. Following Bobby's instructions from earlier tonight, he quickly searches for all of the medical files and emails. While he pulls them up, Goliath takes all the documents we collected and places them on the edge of the desk. Once he's done, we quickly begin untying Jason's feet. We can hear the sounds of the sirens in the distance letting us know it is time to get moving.

Jason is barely conscious when I lean down, just inches from his face and say, "They are going to love a pretty boy like you in prison, especially now that you're missing so many of your fucking teeth." He moans and tugs at the ropes that still hold his hands. "Payback is a bitch, asshole," I say, stepping away from the bed.

Goliath makes one final check of everything we have left for the police, ensuring that they will find what they need to put Jason and his father, along with that other fucked up doctor, in jail for the rest of their lives. We leave there feeling confident that everything will be taken care of. Any two bit local cop would be able to find everything they needed to put him under, but Bishop also notified a few of his contacts, ensuring our protection. With his connections, we won't have to worry about any blowback from everything that went down tonight.

CHAPTER 22

ANA

IT'S BEEN TWO weeks since the night my life spiraled out of control. Doc's phone call to the Medical Board ignited a fire that caused my life as I had always known it to burst into flames and practically combust before my eyes. Everything changed that night. I'm still having a hard time with losing Steven. Honestly, I don't think I will ever get over it, or the fact that it could've been me. A part of me finds comfort in knowing how many lives were saved through all of this, but it's still hard not being able to talk to him. Steven had always been a wonderful friend to me, and I know he'd be happy with the way my life has turned around.

Dillon never would tell me what really happened that night with Jason. He said it was club business, and he couldn't talk about it. I knew he had taken care of it, just like he promised. I wasn't surprised when I read in the newspaper that Jason and his father were arrested. There was a huge investigation, and several doctors and nurses were indicted for organ trafficking. It was over… I had my life back.

Once the news became public, my suspension was lifted from the hospital. They offered to let me come back to work, but I just wasn't interested. That part of my life was over, and I was ready to move on. I decided to take Tessa up on her offer. Doc was able to get me on at the hospital in town, and they even let me keep the hours I had already acquired in Kentucky. I've been working there for several days, and I already love it. The staff is wonderful, and the best part is I get to be with Dillon every day. I couldn't ask for more.

My dad was so relieved to hear that I was back to work. He'd been so worried, and he couldn't be happier with the way everything turned out. It means so much to me that he is okay with me staying here and understands that I need a fresh start. I have no doubt that he will continue to keep a close eye on me. My father is a worrier, and I love him for that.

Dillon called earlier to tell me that he had something to show me after work. I could hear the excitement in his voice, so I am eager to see what he is up to. I go to my locker and change into my jeans and t-shirt. Once I get my boots on, I reach for my Devil Chaser's leather jacket. The smell of fresh leather surrounds me as I slip it on. When I walk down the hall, I get a few questioning looks, but they don't bother me. I love wearing it. It's just another reminder that Dillon is mine, and I'm part of his family now. I've grown to love all of them, and I wear the DC name with pride… having it say Sheppard's property is just an added bonus.

He is sitting on his bike watching me as I walk up to

him. There is just something about seeing that man on a bike. He's so damn hot. His worn blue jeans and boots along with his new Devil Chaser's leather jacket make me painfully aroused. I just can't get enough of him. My heart races when he gets off his bike and starts walking towards me.

"Did you have a good day?" he asks.

"I had a really good day," I tell him just before he leans down to kiss me. I love how his mouth feels against mine, and I immediately feel the loss when he pulls away from me.

"We need to get going," he tells me as he takes my hand and leads me over to the bike.

"Where exactly are we going?" I ask.

"You'll see," he says with a sexy smile.

As soon as he gets on, I lift my leg over the seat, and the smell of his cologne mixed with leather swirls around me as I get settled in my spot. I never thought I'd be one to like riding on a motorcycle, but I love it. The wind whipping around me makes me feel like I'm actually a part of the nature that surrounds us. As soon as he starts the engine, I wrap my arms around his waist and snuggle in close to him.

We've only driven a few miles when he pulls onto an old country road. Beautiful yellow buttercups are sprouting up everywhere, and the dogwood trees are starting to bloom. It's simply breathtaking. He slows down in front of a large log cabin house and pulls into the driveway.

"Come on," he says as he kills the engine and gets

off. He reaches out his hand to help me.

"This place is beautiful, Dillon, but why are we here?" I ask.

"You ask too many questions, Angel," he says as he tugs my hand, leading me up to the front door. He pushes a few buttons on the keypad, and the lock on the door springs open. He smiles as he opens the door. "Go check it out."

I step through the doorway, and I am blown away. It's absolutely amazing. The vintage log cabin theme runs throughout the entire house, with cathedral ceilings and unbelievably tall windows. The awesome view of the lake is the first thing that catches my attention, drawing me into the living room. The trees are all sprouting blooms, and the sun is reflecting off of the lake. It's stunning.

"Dillon, I love it," I tell him.

"We have two other places to check out, but I wanted to show you this one first."

He's so damn cute when he's excited like this. He reminds me of a child on Christmas morning. He walks over to me at the window and stares out onto the lake. He looks so happy, and I can tell he loves it here. "What's going on? Why are you showing me all this?"

"As much as I love the clubhouse, I want us to have a home, so I called a realtor. It's time for us to find a place of our own."

"We're buying a house?" I ask.

"Yeah… and as soon as you tell me which one of them you like, I'll buy it," he says as he leans down and kisses me on the forehead. "After we see the other two places, you can...."

"I want this one," I tell him.

"You haven't seen the others yet."

"I don't have to. This place is perfect," I tell him, smiling. "It's everything I've ever dreamed of and more."

"I was hoping that you'd say that." He slips his arms around my waist, lifting me up into his arms. I wrap my legs around his waist as his mouth crashes against mine. It's hard for me to imagine ever loving him more than I do at this moment. He's already given me so much, and now here he is giving me *more*.

I look up to him and say, "I love it."

"Let's go look at the rest of it," he says as he slowly drops my feet to the floor.

We spend the next hour going through every room in the house, talking about what furniture we'd need and where to put it. There are three bedrooms, so we'll have plenty of room to start a family whenever we get ready. There's even a wraparound porch lined with a gorgeous view of the lake. I can just imagine how great it will be to have my coffee out there every morning.

"You sure this is the one you want? We can go see the others...."

"It's perfect, Dillon."

"Six months," he tells me.

"What do you mean six months?"

"Six months to get things settled here and finish up your residency, then I want to start our family," he says as steps closer to me. "Want to fill this house with our kids. That gonna work for you?"

"Yes, that will work for me," I say, laughing. I wrap my arms around his neck and before I kiss him, I say, "Thank you, Dillon."

CHAPTER 23

SHEPPARD

"WE GOT THAT new shipment in today. There's a 1967 Harley Davidson Electra Glide, and she's a real beauty," Otis tells me. We're sitting in the hotel bar having a drink, watching all the girls run back and forth as they get ready.

"You calling dibs on it?" I ask, laughing.

"Nah, I know better than that. You'll end up finding a way to get it anyway," he tells me as he stands up and straightens his tie. "We better get out there. Bishop's wound pretty tight. Don't wanna be late."

"No doubt," I say as I follow him out the door to the back patio of the Paris Landing Inn.

I have to admit... it looks pretty fucking amazing. Bishop's been planning this wedding for weeks, and it turned out better than any of us ever imagined. There are rows of white covered chairs leading up to a custom made gazebo that's facing the lake. Bouquets of wildflowers are placed on all of the tables and all around the gazebo. Bishop is standing up front with the minister, and the guests are taking their seats.

When we walk up, he says, "It's about time you two showed up."

"We're ten minutes early, brother," I say, smiling. "You look good in your monkey suit." The rest of us are wearing slacks and our DC's leather jackets, but Tessa wanted him to wear a tux. It took her a little convincing, but she managed to talk him into it. She also talked us into wearing a tie, but that's where we drew the line.

"I don't wanna hear it, Shep," Bishop says as he searches the crowd for Tessa.

"It won't be much longer," I whisper as the music begins to play.

Myles and Drake are already standing beside Bishop, both sharing the role of best man. All heads turn when Izzie starts walking towards us. She looks so much like her mother, and everyone smiles as they watch her drop little pink rose petals with each step she takes. When the music changes, the women begin walking down the aisle. Ana was surprised but excited when Tessa asked her to be a bridesmaid. She looks absolutely stunning in the long black dress Tessa picked out. It barely touches the ground as she walk towards us, and the deep V-neck shows just enough skin to be sexy as fuck. My woman looks amazing. Her eyes sparkle when she passes me, and I can't take my eyes off of her.

The music changes again, and Tessa steps out on the terrace with her dad. Tessa is a beautiful bride. She's wearing a simple white dress, and she's holding a large bouquet of pink roses. Bishop is totally captivated by her as she walks down the aisle. All eyes are focused on them when the ceremony begins. As soon as Tessa starts talking about how much Bishop means to her and the kids, Ana glances over to me, making my heart twist in knots. I find myself wondering what kind of wedding Ana and I will have. I never thought I'd be the kind of man that would ever get married, but Ana has changed that. It's going to happen. I'm going to marry her… and soon.

When the ceremony is over, we all gather in one of the banquet halls. It's not exactly fancy, but it's a perfect place for the reception. There is a huge spread of food and a full bar, and everyone seems to be having a good time.

"Hey there, handsome," Ana says as she slips her arms around my waist. With just the touch of her hand, I find myself fighting the urge to have my way with her right there.

"There's my girl." I pull her close and ask, "You ready to get out of here?"

She smiles as she playfully rolls her eyes. "We can't go yet. They haven't even cut the cake."

"You're killing me with that dress, babe." I lean in closer and whisper, "Since the moment I saw you in it, all I've been able to think about is getting you out of it."

"One hour. Then, you can do whatever you want with the dress," she whispers playfully in my ear.

"Deal."

During my darkest moment, she was the light beckoning me back to life. When I look at her, I see my future… my entire life unfolding before my eyes. She's mine. Now and forever.

FROM THE AUTHOR

I can't tell you how much I've enjoyed writing the Devil Chasers' series. These characters have become such a huge part of my life, and I'm finding it difficult to let them go. So, I will let the story continue in that fantasy world I've created in my crazy head.

I'd like to let myself believe that when I drive through Paris, Tennessee, I might come across Bishop and the guys having a drink at Hidden Creek. Or maybe I'll see them riding across the Paris Landing Bridge as they head back to the clubhouse. I might have to fight the urge to follow them! And who knows? Maybe Levi and Conner are hanging out at Matt's Pub, just waiting to buy one of us drink.

Even though this is the end of this series, it doesn't mean you won't be seeing them again. I am really excited about writing Maverick's story. So many of my readers have asked about him, and I want to give him the book that he and my readers deserve. Be prepared for some surprises. His club is quite different from the Devil Chasers, and there will be several shocks along the way. Thank you all again for reading my books. I hope you have enjoyed reading them as much I have enjoyed writing them.

ACKNOWLEDGEMENTS

There are so many people that I'd like to thank for helping me with this book, but no one has been more supportive than Marci Ponce. She's been there every step of the way, helping me any way she could. She will never know how much her help has meant to me. Thank you Marci for being my guiding light through this series and helping me stay on track. You are a wonderful writer and friend.

I would also like to thank all of my readers. I have loved all of your comments and posts. I am blown away every time I see one of your comments about liking my books. It blows me away! When my life has gotten a little crazy, your kind words have given me the encouragement I've needed to continue on.

My Wilder's Women Street Team is amazing! Thank you all for your support. It means so much to me that you continue to help me with reviews and posting all of my teasers. You all rock! There are too many names to mention here but know that I love you all.

My Beta readers are Rock Stars!! Erin, Patricia, Sherri, Keeana, Terra, Jenny, Danielle, Kimberely, Elizabeth, and Brandy, you guys rock!! Thanks so much for taking the time to read *Combust* and posting your reviews. Your reviews and comments mean so much to me!!

I want to give a special thank you to Jess Peterson and Jane Mortensen for all your help with creating my teasers. You both are so creative, and I love your work. Thanks for always being there when I need you. Jane Mortensen has made incredible trailers for each of my books. Be sure to check out my Facebook page to see them all.

Jess Peterson's Page: (She's awesome by the way)
www.facebook.com/events/381121918727263/382627968576658/

Jane Mortensen's Page:
www.facebook.com/jam47?fref=ts

Jordan Marie, you're an amazing author and friend. Thank you for all of your encouragement, and I can't wait to read your next book!

Ana Rosso, my young grasshopper, I hope you have enjoyed this book. Your input was wonderful. I hope it lived up to all of your expectations. You are such a wonderful friend!!! Keep on rocking chickeroo!!

A final thanks to my editor, Brooke Asher. You are amazing. Thank you for taking the time to make my books the best that they can be. You are such a wonderful friend and editor. Thank you for all the wonderful things you do.

Brooke's Page:
www.facebook.com/profile.php?id=100008407952883&fref=ts

FYI: If you like MC Romances, you should check out Autumn Jones Lake. Her books are wonderful!

www.facebook.com/autumnjlake?fref=ts

★ Devil Chaser's MC Series ★

Inferno

Smolder

Ignite

Consumed

Excerpt from

INFERNO

A Devil Chaser's MC Romance

PROLOGUE

THE LOUD CRASH of a bottle breaking against the wall startled Myles as he walked up to his dad's bike garage. It was late, and he wasn't expecting anyone to be there. His dad had sent him to grab his backpack that he'd left there after school. As he got closer, he heard male voices coming from the rear of the building.

"You better get this shit settled with Bishop. The shipment is due in Memphis by the end of the week, and I expect it to be there!"

This was an unfamiliar voice. As he looked in the garage window, Myles didn't recognize the man, but he knew he was furious. It made him even more uneasy when he heard Goliath's heated tone. Goliath was the Devil Chaser's VP, and he was not someone you wanted to piss off.

"What the hell are you thinking, Duce? You know this isn't the way to handle this. If you have a problem, you take it up with Bishop. You do *not* show up unannounced and try to conduct business behind his back. This shit isn't right."

"He's been putting me off. I know something's up. I'm giving you a chance to fix it before I have to handle things myself. If Bishop can't get this shit done, he'll be taken out and replaced with someone who can."

Goliath shouted, "Are you seriously threatening our President? I know you've got these gangs giving you trouble, but you don't wanna go there, man. You don't come here and make threats without consequences."

"I expect my goddamn shipment to be made by the end of the week. Either Bishop steps up and gets shit done, or he's out. No explanation necessary!" the stranger shouted.

Goliath moved towards him with fire in his eyes and snarled, "The shipment will be there. But this shit here tonight does not fly, asshole. Bishop *will* hear about it, and he'll expect a meet with you. Plan on it."

MYLES QUICKLY TURNED and headed back home. This encounter definitely had him freaking out. At only eleven, he'd already had to deal with a lot. After his mother, Cassie, left when he was just four, his dad and the club had been the only family he'd known. His father, Bishop, was the President of the Devil Chasers MC. His dad was an exceptional leader who always thought three steps ahead. His men trusted him and knew that he would lead them with conviction. Bishop believed in his brotherhood, and he was an inspiration to those that followed him. Goliath had been his vice-president for three years and helped communicate the expectations of the club. The Sergeant of Arms, Ace, had been in office for four years and led with an iron fist. He kept the meetings under control and handled any outside issues that came up with the club. Sheppard, Renegade, Pops, Hag, Crack Nut Bobby, and Doc had been members since the club began ten years ago. There were two prospects, Otis and Bulldog, still waiting to get patched in. When Cassie left, these men and several of their old ladies had become Myles's family, and the clubhouse had become his second home.

Things had been going pretty well for Myles until Cassie had returned after two years hoping to start things back up like she had never left. Myles had known his dad didn't really like that she was back, but he had tried to hide it for Myles's sake. Bishop had wanted him to have his mother, and Myles had actually liked having her back. It had made him feel better knowing that his mother wanted him again. Unfortunately, she just couldn't get her act together. She loved to party and hooked up with different men in and out of the club. She always seemed to be looking for something more. Eventually, one night of partying had gotten out of control, and she'd ended up dead. Myles still didn't know all the details, but he knew it had pissed his dad off even more.

The conversation he'd just overheard in the garage worried him. Was his dad's life in danger? Would Goliath protect him? Goliath was a big dude, and no one messed with him unless you wanted to get a fist in the face.

CHAPTER 1

TESSA

"YOU KNOW IDIOMS are just phrases that people use to add humor to conversation. They aren't meant to be taken literally. Actually, you use them all the time. I often hear you all talking about 'checking' each other. When you say, 'Laurie was checking me', it doesn't mean she's actually putting a check mark on you. You know it means that she is saying bad things about someone."

Tessa had been a 5th grade teacher at Henry County Elementary for almost two years. She loved teaching, and she always felt that she learned more from her students than they learned from her. She had moved to Paris, Tennessee with her two children, Isabelle and Drake, shortly after her divorce. She needed a change of scenery for her family, and the move had been a good choice for them. She had visited Paris Landing as a child, and had always loved being at the lake. She had been excited to come back, and she'd needed the distance from her overbearing ex-husband. Her marriage had not been a happy one, and she'd wanted a new start for her kids. The schools in Paris were some of the best in the area, and she'd been glad to get a teaching position there.

DANIEL SAID, "LIKE 'skating on thin ice' doesn't mean that you're really skating on ice. It really means you're about to get in so much trouble!"

"That's right, Daniel. Does anyone else have an idiom to share?" Tessa asked.

"How about 'hot, hot like a tater tot'? That doesn't mean you feel hot. It means you *are* HOT! Good looking! Smoking… You know, HAWT!" Lindsey shouted from the back of the classroom.

"Yes, that could work. Actually, that one is pretty good, Lindsey. Anyone else?"

"Mom told my dad to 'break a leg' last week when he had to go to a big meeting at work. I don't think she meant it, though," Luke added.

"You're right, Luke, that means good luck. That's an old one. Not really sure how someone came up with that," Tessa chuckled.

Bradley, a known troublemaker in the class, turned to face Myles and said viciously, "I'd like to 'knock you into next week'. That would work, wouldn't it, Ms. Campbell?" He smirked at Myles.

Myles immediately jumped out of his seat and began punching Bradley in the face, shoulder, and back. Bradley tried to tuck his head in towards his desk, as Myles shouted, "How 'bout I 'high five your *face*'?!" He kept hitting Bradley as Tessa scrambled to the back of the room.

"Myles Bishop, stop that right now! What are you

thinking?" Tessa screeched. Myles popped Bradley one more time on the side of his face, and Tessa lost her temper. "Myles! I. SAID. STOP!" She pulled Myles from Bradley and led him out of the classroom and into the hall.

"Before you start yelling, Ms. Campbell, he was asking for it! He's such an idiot. I can't stand that fucker!" Myles shouted.

"Language, Myles! And there's no excuse for laying into him like that. You know I have to write you up now.... Your dad will have to be called, and I'm sure the principal will want to suspend you. You're too smart for this. I expected more from you," Tessa said with concern.

Tessa hated to see Myles get in any trouble. Yes, he was wrong to hit Bradley, but she knew that kid was a jerk. He'd caused issues with several of her students, and she was tired of dealing with him. Seeing the worry in Myles's eyes only made it worse. His shaggy brown hair trimmed his angelic face, and his dark brown eyes pleaded with her to understand. He wasn't exactly small for his age, but he seemed so vulnerable. God she hated dealing with this part of her job.

"I'm sorry, Ms. Campbell. I just couldn't let him get away with that. He really is a jerk face, and you know he's a pain.... Hey, did you like my idiom? You gotta admit it was pretty good, right? 'High five your ***face***'!" Myles said with a smile.

"Don't go there, Myles. This isn't funny. Stay here while I get an assistant to watch the class. We have to go see the principal." Tessa did her best to hold back her smile. He was right, that was a pretty good one. She might have to use it sometime.

As they made their way to the office, Myles was quiet. Tessa knew he was worried about facing the principal, and he probably wasn't all that happy about seeing his dad afterwards. She put her hand on his shoulder and guided him in.

The secretary called Tessa and Myles into Principal Morrison's office. He sat behind his large walnut desk that was too big for the small room. He was in his early fifties and wore a navy business suit. His rotund build reminded her of the dad from *Family Guy*. As she walked in, he gave her a wide leering smile that gave her the creeps. She still hadn't gotten used to the way he checked her out every time she walked by. He obviously had a thing for curvy girls, and he didn't mind letting her know it.

"To what do I owe the pleasure, Ms. Campbell? You are looking *very* well today," Principal Morrison said, his gaze loitering on her chest as he spoke.

Tessa cleared her throat in hopes of getting his attention to her eyes instead of her boobs. It didn't work.

"Thank you, Mr. Morrison. Unfortunately, Myles is in a bit of trouble. He hit Bradley several times in class today. I wouldn't really consider it a fight, because Bradley didn't get a chance to hit him back."

Morrison spoke firmly and never even looked at Myles, "Call his dad in. You can decide on a fair punishment, since it happened in your class. Make sure he knows that he'll deal with me if it happens again. Is that all I can help you with today? Maybe you would like to meet for dinner tonight so we can discuss the school fair next month?"

"Thanks for the offer, but I'm really busy. I have tons of papers to grade. I'll call his dad in, and we'll work something out. Thanks for your time. I'll let you know what we plan to do." Tessa smiled and slipped out of his office before he could say anything else. Myles followed her quietly out the door. She pointed to one of the seats in front of the office. Myles sat and waited for her.

Now, she had to make *the* phone call. This was another part of her job that she wasn't crazy about. She really thought a lot of Myles, and she was worried about him. One minute he seemed perfectly happy, and the next, his temper would flare. On more than one occasion, he had argued with students in the class. He was often quiet, and he didn't contribute to their classroom discussions. There were those days that he seemed to be a regular, happy fifth grader, but other times, he seemed to be lost in his own world. Maybe there was something going on with him. Hopefully his dad would be willing to help figure it out.

Made in the USA
Lexington, KY
26 July 2015